9.

D0891283

Men Die

H. L. Humes

MEN DIE

A Novel

Random House Trade Paperbacks

New York

For ALH
Empress of All My Country
& for K & JNB
Who Cheered Her Musicians

"... And if the Captain ask you,
Tell him I'm going.
Tell him I'm gone.

If he ask you was I laughing,
Tell him I was cryin'.

Tell him I'm gone ..."

Leadbelly

INTRODUCTION
Alan Cheuse

As much as I would like to offer a thoroughly persuasive and wholly sound critical appraisal of these two novels by Harold "Doc" Humes, one of the least-known and most enigmatic members of his writing generation, I won't be able to speak about the books without first explaining how they intertwined with my own education. Or more precisely, how they became *part* of my education, in the way that some fine (or sometimes merely ordinary) books often do during that special phase in your life when raw minutes and art bind together in what, years later, you might recognize as the first blush of vocation.

I was completing my sophomore year at Rutgers and had taken over the editorship of the literary magazine, *The Anthologist,* from a fellow named James Shokoff (whose whereabouts today I sometimes wonder about) when William Sloane, who directed the Bread Loaf Writers' Conference with another teacher of mine, John Ciardi, offered me and a few others the chance to wait tables at the workshop that summer of 1958. We drove up to Vermont and carried trays for various famous writers and not-so-famous editors. One of them, a trim, dark-haired woman named Mary Heathcote, became a friend to the tall, stoop-shouldered, enthusiastic would-be bohemian that I was.

That autumn she invited me and a few other Rutgers boys to parties at her apartment in Greenwich Village. At one of these pleasant little fiestas, I met a chunk-boned, jocular man a little shorter than me, with his lovely wife and some small children in arms. He turned out to be Harold Humes, a founder of the *Paris Review,* recently returned from a long postwar sojourn in Europe. His first novel, *The Underground City,* had just been published in New York. Unlike the work of some of the other writers I had met that summer (Norman Mailer, Ralph Ellison, and Richard Yates, among others), Humes' fiction was unknown to me. Mary Heathcote sent me a copy of his massive book; I put aside my regular reading (an act *not* unknown to me in my student years) and spent some days in my dustbin of an apartment a few blocks from the Rutgers campus in dilapidated New Brunswick, New Jersey, feasting on Humes' story of politics and the disasters of war and love and peace and paternity in France circa 1944–47.

That year—in the spring of 1959—we inaugurated a regular reading series by accomplished visiting writers, something that we take for granted as part of an undergraduate literature education these days. But in the late fifties and early sixties it was a trick that we had to learn to do by trying it out. With a little financial help and a lot of encouragement from a few sympathetic instructors in the Rutgers English department, those of us on the magazine staff invited Yates (who came to read), Mailer (who did not), Ciardi (who was already in place), and a few others, including Harold Humes.

Humes showed up. In the front room of a splendid nineteenth-century townhouse appropriated by the university years before and with book in hand, he read vigorously from *The Underground City*. Head bobbing, arms waving, he looked like a middleweight boxer with his fight strategy in front of him. He then led a question-and-answer period about modern writing.

"Let me ask *you* a question," he said to the audience. "How many of you"—there were about forty of us in the crowd before him, mostly students, a few faculty members including John

McCormick (critic, bullfight expert, and biographer), and Ciardi and Sloane—"have read a book called *Under the Volcano*?"

McCormick's hand shot up. Mine did, too, except that I hadn't read it, though as was often the case with my education in those days I found a copy of the novel and took care of that deficiency in my life soon after.

"Three of us!" Humes chuckled. "Three good readers. The rest of you will remain flawed until you know that novel. Not damaged. But flawed somewhat. You're missing out on a great feast, a great fiesta of human frailty and extraordinary writing."

Talk about frailty—the next season saw Humes publish his second and only other novel, *Men Die,* a book as compact in its genius as *The Underground City* was huge and overbearing. Then he seemed to disappear from the New York scene. One heard rumors that he was experimenting with a new drug called LSD—and later in the decade I read accounts in the New York press that he was seen distributing five-dollar bills to crowds at the entrance to Columbia University. A scheme of his for building houses out of paper drew a write-up in *The New York Times.* But no more fiction came from him.

I encountered him again in Bennington, Vermont, in the early seventies. I was teaching there and one of his daughters was a student. Humes seemed to have made himself over into a character from a novel in progress. He was a graying, shambling wrack of paranoia and good cheer, talking of a massage cure for heroin addicts, which he had tried to promote in Italy and the United States, and explaining that it was well understood in certain circles that the CIA could monitor the progress of radical dissidents, of whom he was one, from seemingly innocuous clouds that traveled above them on roadways across the country. He bunked in his daughter's dormitory. Students gathered around him. They had just read *The Rime of the Ancient Mariner,* and here was the mariner in the flesh.

I never saw Humes again after his Bennington visitations, but fifteen years later his remark about Malcolm Lowry's work came to mind when, invited by David Madden to contribute to the second of his "Rediscoveries" volumes, I chose Humes' books as the fiction I thought ought to come back into print. I discovered upon rereading them that he made rare books in the best sense, great feasts and fiestas, and my reencounters with them convinced me that in the raw, instinctual days of early recognitions, my admiration for Humes' writing was not at all misplaced. I recommended them at nineteen because I found the books thrilling in ways that I could not at the time explain. In my late forties, I found them just as thrilling, and in addition I could muster a few ideas as to why.

The Underground City stands as one of those rare birds of American fiction, a true novel of ideas with credible characters and a powerful realistic plot. Humes divides the book into three large chunks, and by the way he sets his first scene, with a vast canvas of cloud and sky above Paris at the opening of a day about a year or so following the end of World War II, he seems to have nothing less in mind than the desire to create a monumental story of epic range:

> The eastern sun, full and fiery orange, just risen clear of the horizon, began slowly to sink back into the gray ocean of clouds as the plane started down; the sky altered; clouds changed aspects. To the southeast, delicate as frozen breath, an icy herd of mare's tails rode high and sparkling in the upper light of the vanishing sun; they were veiled in crystalline haze as the plane descended through stratocirrus, the sun in iridescent halo at its disappearing upper limb. And below, slowly rising closer, the soft floor of carpeting clouds gradually changed into an ugly boil of endless gray

billows, ominous, huge. Against the east, rayed out in a vast
standing fan: five fingers of the plummeting sun. . . .

That airplane carries the crippled and ailing American ambassador to France, the portentously named Bruce Peel Sheppard,
back to Paris after a medical leave, in order to deal with an im-
pending crisis: the war-crimes trial of a collaborator named Du-
jardin, whose case the French Communist Party has just taken
up—on the side of the supposed war criminal—as a way of at-
tacking the U.S. presence in postwar Europe. Caught in the
middle of this rising political storm is New Jersey–born John
Stone, a heroic but now burned-out alcoholic American undercover agent. Under the code-name "Dante," Stone led a group
of commandos who smuggled arms to the French Resistance in
advance of the Allied invasion. Stone, appropriately enough,
now works in the civilian wing of the U.S. embassy under the
guise of a graves registration official. As Ambassador Peel's
aircraft prepares to make its descent below the clouds into what
Humes, with deliberate homage to Andre Malraux (author of
that great novel of ideas, *Man's Fate*) calls "the world of men,"
we encounter a broad cast of characters and become engaged in
a masterly setup for a dramatization of the world of modern
Western geopolitical affairs. Just as the trial will rip open the
wounds on the French body politic still fresh from the war, the
large central portion of the novel gives us the narrative of
Stone's undercover work during the war—a dense, dramatic
novel within the novel that may be the best story of the Resistance told by anyone in English (which stands as the testimony
Stone will give at the trial of the accused and contentious Du-
jardin). The last third of the novel shows us the aftermath of the
trial, and the unfolding fates of Ambassador Sheppard, Stone, a
Resistance leader named Merseault, the Communists Picard

and Carnot, and a number of other characters involved in the wartime and postwar drama.

Humes' treatment of the military and political aspects of the events alone would have been brilliant enough, but he undergirds these public matters with the burning psychology of personal motives, stories of lost sons and troubled fathers that involve both Ambassador Sheppard and Stone, as well as a mysterious member of the Resistance code-named Berger (again Humes plays tribute to Malraux by using the writer's own wartime code name). There is, too, a philosophical level to the book: the presentation of a number of warring views of history and politics, from the ill-fated notions of the ambassador on through the paranoid psycho-historical theories of the Communist manipulator Picard (which, as critic James Bloom pointed out in the original version of a brief note on Humes—perhaps the only critical notice that the book has received in the thirty years since its publication—portends the now-fashionable strategies of paranoiac fiction as exemplified by the work of Thomas Pynchon). Moreover, there is a rich mythological overlay to the story, beginning with the ambassador's descent from the heavens at the beginning of the book, on through the central return back in time to the years of the Resistance in the Stone narrative—as well as a lot of seeming counterparts to figures out of European poetry and myth among various characters, including Stone ("Dante") who makes his physical descent into the underworld of the sewers in the final section of the novel.

If *The Underground City* appears, deceptively at first, to be one of those loose and baggy monsters of which Henry James complained, the compactness of *Men Die,* published less than a year later, might give the initial impression of simplistic storytelling about a complex period: the months leading up to the United States' entry into the Pacific War. *The Underground City* seems almost wholly anomalous in its essence, a work that no other American writer tried to write before Humes (except for the neophyte attempt of Humes' *Paris Review* compatriot Peter Matthiessen, whose now deservedly forgotten early novel, *Partisans,* unlike his triumphant later work, comes nowhere near the success of Humes' book). *Men Die* has a number of echoes and companion works, beginning with James Jones' *From Here to Eternity,* Warren Eyster's (equally) ignored *Far From the Customary Skies,* William Styron's novella *The Long March,* and George Garrett's *Which Ones are the Enemy?*—these last two being, of course, books with postwar settings.

Men Die is set in a United States–occupied Caribbean island that has been carved out into a honeycomb of tunnels by a battalion of black navy laborers in anticipation of the outbreak of World War II. Lording over the operation is Commander Bonuso Hake, a Captain Queeg–like figure who fascinates young Lieutenant Everett Sulgrave, the officer in charge of the actual tunneling and stockpiling operations. Ben Dolfuss, Hake's former first in command, is the third white man on the island. He appears to have had an affair with Vannessa Hake, the commander's sensual wife. The entire narrative explodes at the outset as the ammunition dump goes sky-high, leaving alive only Sulgrave and six black mutineers, who piece together the corpse of the commander—and the story of his life and command. Thus the novel itself is a series of highly charged narrative fragments that take us back and forth in time, from Hake's assumption of command on through the explosion, the funeral of Hake in Washington, and Sulgrave's pathetic love affair with Vannessa. Some sections include overtly stream-of-consciousness vignettes from the untimely widowed Vannessa's point of view.

With all this you might think that the book itself was a disaster, as though James Jones had never recovered from a reading of *The Sound and the Fury.* But Humes' novel is tersely and convincingly composed, and while it echoes other works it

xv

never seems derivative, the result perhaps of its powerfully made scenes (such as a fire drill on the arsenal island in which a fire hose takes on a life of its own and nearly kills some men) and the essentially clear and direct nature of Humes' prose. Fathers searching for sons, sons looking for fathers, and a military structure destroying that which it is meant to defend: These are some of the motifs from Humes' first novel that we notice at work again in this second book. In the philosophical musings of the slightly demented Commander Hake we find some of the paranoid theories of *The Underground City* emerging as a prelude for war in another theater (and clearly echoing some of the chords struck by Mailer in his portrayal of the commanding general in *The Naked and the Dead*). *Men Die* is a finely executed, dramatic curtain raiser to the great story of the war, whose last year and aftermath Humes himself portrays with such breadth in his earlier novel.

It is nearly fifty years later, and now both books have come back into print. It remains unclear to me why they ever disappeared, except that perhaps when Humes himself went, in his own way, "underground," there was no one else partisan enough to lobby on behalf of further editions. Taken together they show the hand of a writer whose inventive projections and first-rate narratives deserve to see the light of day again. These books hold up the way *Under the Volcano* holds up. Until you read them, as Humes himself remarked to us all those many decades ago about the Lowry novel, "you will remain flawed. Not damaged. But flawed somewhat. You're missing out on a great feast, a great fiesta of human frailty and extraordinary writing."

Men Die

When the blast finally came it came foreseen, like the end of the world. In a shuddering chamber of solid rock the walls shook as though swayed in a windstorm; seven men were sprinkled with chunks of rock and ashen dust from the ceiling of their underground bunker. Instantly they knew that outside, men were dying: knew with a certainty that comes only from having imagined the event a thousand times; from having lived with it, in dreams, daytime nightmares; from having expected it, waited for it even; from having almost come to look forward to an end—whatever end—to suspense, daily monotony, fear. But even then none of them could foresee that they, six black prisoners and their white warder, would be the only beings left alive on Manacle Shoal Rock. Outside, over the entire lee side of the island, even the birds were already dead.

After the first blast—more a series of blasts, a sustained shaking of the earth—in the first brief astonishment of silence, Lieutenant Junior Grade Everett Turner Sulgrave, USNR, self-appointed warder of the six mutineers, put down the ladle with which he was doling out the noontime beef stew, and said NO God no.

Fireman First Class Randolph Handy, who had a brother outside, slammed down his mess gear and said Lord Lord I knew it; barechested and black, he sat down on an empty fifty-caliber ammunition box, put his head in his hands, and cried. The raging sound of grief was shocking in that incredible space of sifting dust and silence; the others simply stared, immobile in the downdrifting dust that settled

3

whitely into close black hair and about bare black shoulders. Lieutenant Sulgrave, white, uncertain and very young, said Maybe your brother wasn't on the pier, and Big Randy looked up bitterly and laughed, a snort of tender contempt for weak-sighted whitefolks sympathy: You go on believing it, whiteboy. And that was all that was said until the Lieutenant unlocked the iron gate to the bunker and the ammunition ship went up where it had been unloading in the harbor below: he unlocked the gate and stood framed in the opening an instant, blasted with silent white, blazing, blinding light, silent only for that arrested instant of surprise, followed by a roaring wall of heat and sound, a concussive punch that slammed him down like a rag doll into the dust. The Lieutenant rolled sideways out of the doorway and staggered up, groaning from having the breath knocked out of him, fell again, dragged clear of the door just as another paralyzing blast shook loose more rocks from the ceiling. The prisoners, except Randy, ducked into the corners in fear that the roof would collapse under the trembling tons of rock in the hillside above the bunker. Randy still sat apparently untouched or unreached by the buffeting concussions, his black face illumined with each successive flash. Outside, debris was starting to fall, hot shards of metal, smoking chunks of stone and steel and timber that clanged and thudded off the rock-and-concrete bunker like cosmic hail. Explosion followed explosion in the bunkers and tunnels below; the rocking earth cracked and rumbled.

Finally rumbling ceased, cracking and quivering ceased, and there was only the steady rainfall thud of debris; then the silence, the sky black, the noon sun a dull red orb through the cataclysmic dust.

When they came out they saw what hell had been: the piers and buildings were no more, and the fifteen-thousand-ton ammunition ship that had been unloading was vanished to nowhere. The turquoise water of the bay was milky with pulverized coral.

First to find the living: there were none. Find then the first among the dead. Find then the Commander. Bonuso Severn Hake, Commander, USN.

Nightfall. Walking eyedeep in hell amid fires, occasional explosions, they heard the plane sent from San Juan, a hundred miles away; the blast had broken windows there. The Commander was already assembled in a box when the plane arrived, a PBY amphibian that circled like a carrion bird before settling to the blackened corpse.

Lieutenant Everett Turner Sulgrave, determined to search again for life or movement, had left the Commander's remains to the six black victims of his wrath; the prisoners had dragged through the bloody wreckage until Schoolboy and Lace found the head and shoulders. In the spillage of a ruptured sea chest Big Randy grimly rummaged until he found what Orval BlueEyes said was there: a clean set of dress whites, the Commander's best. His famous sword wasn't found till later. The body was assembled for transport—the suit held Bonuso Hake together—in a makeshift coffin, a shipping crate stenciled in black: DELICATE OPTICAL INSTRUMENTS ** STORE AWAY FROM BOILERS. And that is how he was flown out—in accordance with his drunken wish, once stated to Sulgrave—to be returned to the river of Annapolis, Severn, which name he bore.

It was dusk when Sulgrave came and briefly inspected the body before ordering the hasty coffin nailed shut. He had tears in his eyes, even though he had nearly hated this flesh. But he had found the Commander's wife's letters, and in a frenzied, almost religious necessity to understand the significance of his death, had begun their reading. For the last two hours he had sat among the spill of the Commander's belongings reading. He read until the light failed, then went to see the body, one letter still in hand. In the other he carried the red leather box, once upon a happier time a gift of love, embossed with gilt: LETTERS FROM VANNA.

They closed and sealed the crate, heard the plane before they saw it. They all looked at each other, taking stock of themselves for the first time, six black enlisted men and the one white officer, saw that they were all marked with his, the dead Commander's, dried blood.

Big Randy spoke first, not deliberately, but musing. "They know outside about us?"

Lieutenant Everett Turner Sulgrave, USNR, nodded. "Put you down as ringleader."

Poke said, "Mutiny. Shee-it." Disgust, not rancor.

"That could buy you twenty years, man," said Orval BlueEyes, who had been the Commander's steward. "You lucky it's peacetime yet."

"Shee-it, man," Poke said. "You can do twenty standin' on one foot."

"I got my money on you, man," Lace said.

Digger Marples shook his head and laughed, bitter, and looked at the mute box, at the STORE AWAY FROM BOILERS. "You pore ridic'less daid sonuvabitch," he said. "We still gonna have to live with you."

funeral
his deathday party
thirty minutes I go downstairs   still alive
I am still alive   I am
Vannessa Lee Lynch Hake   38   lying abed naked
could have been a better wife to him   *true or false*
  Staring at ceiling

                                            Unfamiliar   ciel
bleu   egg and dart   Egganddart Hotel   *true*
won't listen to this   won't listen   *yes   true*
could have been a better husband damn his lovely
  I am   *He's gone*
Beautiful   they tell me   stunning   they tell me
  oh his baroness   *really really gone*
movie star   he told me   he told me
Now he's gone   *really really really gone*
                              dead   they tell me oh
damn him   damn him   damn him oh damn him   damn
damn his dead eyes   *poor lovely dead eyes   love*
  him   *oh him him him him him*
  Rollover smell of hotel sheets soothing and
smoothing   tears stick   starched sheets and
clean pillow   pillows   two pillows
one for my *belly one* for my head none for the
little boy who killed himself dead   *gone*
                                          gone gone gone

  get used to he's gone
  in thirty minutes I go downstairs

dirty ugly word funeral   *body body who*
delivery of the body   who will arrange
    in transit   *in delivery*
sic transit   Call my young man
    all staff and no rod to comfort me
                              ten hours bearing down

(There is a disconnected scene which also haunts her,
minor-keyed, evoked by memory of other funerals: remembered fragments float into mind; of being thrashed by her
husband with a razor strop; and of her father, the old dead
Admiral, who beat her once for wearing lipstick, at sixteen,
a week after her mother's funeral. Sharp memories. In fury
and in guilt and in helplessness, she rises naked from the bed
and goes to the door. Locks it. Returns to bed, a secret person, and cries. Alone, full of love, she lies on her back, one
pillow over her eyes, and locks her pillowed wrists between
her legs. Rigid as lonely death, she re-enacts the furious
scene, the shattering erotic dream, piecing together memories
in her shuttered mind like shards of a smashed mirror. Lost in
the lonely cycle of that mystery and that longing, she imag-
ines now the conjunctions of carnal love, the entrances and
withdrawals—still lying perfectly still, lost from time—arches
her back for several minutes, neck rigid, teeth gritted, eyes
blind with tears; is slowly trapped in rhythms of love experienced, in grinding memories of vanished flesh: nearly
faints with the animal force of the final illumination.
    Then, calm, abandoned by incubus but terrified by loneli-
ness, she opens her eyes, mindlessly stares at the ceiling:
    Our Father . . .)

Time to call my lieutenant   go downstairs
widow on his arm   *vulve*

8

Veuve French more genital verve
I'm a veuve   more to the missed point
  I'm too old for scruples too old
oh damn him   why should I   *son*
like son like father   *laboring oh*
born but to die   conceived there at his birthday
picnic by the river   *flowing*
and today I bury oh him   deathday
oh   the father
oh   no more sons
my dead   born on a picnic
  think   *warm no wind*
In thirty minutes   *wild with wanting*
  Escort me sir   *wee rabbit oh*
                  rolled up on my hips sticks and stones
at noon   *hurt my knees oh my sweet*
long ride ahead   *God leaves in my hair*
  Then ate deviled eggs by water
I'm not young now   *oak hips*
Randy old mare   *chestnut breasts*
I'll pray with the rest

                                        arms white birch

can't be smart aleck   I loved him yes
  oh afraid   *wee brer rabbit*
afraid of being alone   *wild goat*
call off my young lieutenant
my sheep and my goat to
  comfort me

                                    oh his son his son

planted his lily in my briar patch
took me   I loved him then   *ram ram*
  on my hands knees oh   *ramming*
    leaves in hair   *ram*

9

fingers curled in   *ram*
  God's black earth oh crammed
home a child is born   *born wet*
  Time to go soon
time to call my young man my proper
young man to take me there   oh damn
need a drink   *true or false*
Sulgrave   odd name   not USN   no
  Oh stop thinking like a navy
wife now   *gone gone gone*
navy widow navy widow   navy veuve
  oh his baroness   good grief
his barrenness   could kill him for
  nothing left behind
        no son   no children
God I never knew I'd grieve him like this
  So full of him   *gone gone*
love the feel of my own flesh   *gone*
so full of him   so empty   *barren*
  Rolling over again

              wet flesh after swimming
belly to the cold sun   by highgate
I raised my knees   There I feel my hands
inside my thighs   legs spread
  thighs   lovely soft word
soft like my skin there
  he said more   he said silken
thighs   silken hair
  and then for Sevie they shaved it
painted me with iodine   *bear down*
damn that accursed nurse   ten hours
          she knew how to get it in
          she knows how to get it out

I should have killed her   *and pain*
  But oh the warm sun   *halt*

                       the warm warm sun

Vanna Hake full of ache
          38   full of hate
  and beautiful   lying here naked
full of grief and full of lust

                         yes all right yes
wallow in the lily pads   *go on*
                 proposed for the deserver
Oh why   good God why   *Our Father*
  non decorum est   *who art in*
all lies to makes us ashamed of loving
  Grief   good God good grief   *in*
grief   relief   relife   *love love*
             relife relive relove oh love love love
                       relust reluct

The day of arrival had been warning enough, or should have been. Approaching the Anegada Passage, the sea was slick and ripe with heat and motionless except for the ship's oily track. Lieutenant Sulgrave passed the afternoon digesting an uneasy lunch, leaned sweating on the taffrail listening to the unchanging oily throb of the Diesels. To the northeast a rain squall slowly makes up, looming out of the horizontal haze like an old woman in rags; for three hours the gray slattern shuffles alongside several miles abaft the port beam, but it is late afternoon before the sun cools and the ship feels the first whiff of her perfume; as though in answer the hull quivers, the Diesels turn up a knot.

That squall turned into two days of weather, and Manacle Shoal turned up out of the gray-hanging rain like an obstacle nearly tripped over rather than a proper destination. The black volcanic rocks looked hellish and forbidding, and the rain was too heavy for anything green to be visible.

In docking the small motor ship, one of the Negro pier hands caught his hand between the bollard and the steel bow line just at the moment of strain; the coxswain slacked off on the foredeck winch instantly but too late, and his mates led the injured man off the pier cradling his destroyed right hand like a fallen bird. The cry of greeting, that incredible shout of animal agony that ripped through the hubbub of the foredeck, was what should have warned him.

Benjamin Dolfus, Lieutenant Senior Grade, USN, was on the dock to meet the small contingent of technicians who accompanied Sulgrave. He took Sulgrave's salute absentmindedly and introduced himself. He had blood on his sleeve from helping free the injured dock hand, and was obviously in no mood for trivial amenities.

"Your gear will be brought ashore and stowed in your quarters, Mister Sulgrave. Unless you have a pressing need for my companionship, I'm going to leave you and go have a drink." He stared morosely out at the rain, at the shrouded sea. "Goddamned rain deadens sound—that boy didn't hear your boatswain. Be lucky if he keeps more than his thumb." Then he looked squarely at Sulgrave, asked, "Why didn't you stay home?"

For no reason, a shudder passed through Sulgrave, a visible shudder; he had a mental vision of the fingerless black hand. Like a man collapsing, or finally remembering to collapse, he dropped his false-face of formal greeting. Dolfus saw it.

"You're—what?—twenty-four?" Dolfus asked.

Sulgrave nodded. "Twenty-three. In a few days."

"Well, you're old enough to drink, anyway. They call me Skully here—" He lifted his rain hat just high enough for Sulgrave to see that he was completely bald. "You may as well join the party."

Though he was bald, Dolfus wasn't old. Sulgrave estimated his age at perhaps forty, old perhaps for his rank; he was probably a mustang, he thought, a man risen through the ranks almost against his will.

"We'll go to the Officers' Club," Dolfus said. "Leave everything right here. Nobody steals anything on an island. At least not my crew." He said my crew with unmistakable pride, and followed the remark with a long look toward the dock, where the stevedores, stripped to the waist and shiny black in the rain, were already unloading packing cases. Then he said, looking hard at Sulgrave, "Everything on this rock is black except you, me, and Admiral God."

13

"Who?"

"Just keep it in mind. You're outnumbered and surrounded. Before you meet the admiral of this unsinkable flagship, I think I'd better take you in hand. I had expected someone with more experience. Your orders, please."

Sulgrave handed over the BUPERS folder with his papers in it. Dolfus weighed it in his palm and said, "Naval ROTC, am I right?"

Sulgrave nodded.

"Bachelor of the Liberal Arts. Yale? Amherst? Harvard?"

"Harvard."

Dolfus raised his eyes heavenward. "Well, let's keep it a secret, all right?"

"Anything you say," Sulgrave said, uncomfortable.

"I've said it."

Manacle Shoal was the name for the small complex of rocks and islands of which Manacle Shoal Rock was the largest. The curiously shaped hourglass reef that protected the islands from the open sea looked on the chart like a pair of handcuffs with the string of islands forming the connecting chain.

The Officers' Club was not on the main island—the "Rock" as it was called by Dolfus—but was reached by flat-bottomed boat from the eastern end. The Commander had ordered that no civilians, native or otherwise, would take up quarters on the Rock; thus the usual community that springs up around a naval base existed on a neighboring island. It was a short jeep ride to the eastern end of the Rock, then two minutes by ferry—a curious bargelike affair that looked like a garbage scow, with an outboard motor that kicked up a spectacular rooster tail as it drove the sluggish craft across the narrow shallow channel. It had a drop-front for driving the jeep on to it. As Dolfus observed, it would have been easier to leave the jeep, but for the drenching rain.

There were few comforts among the pleasures of Little Misery—Dolfus informed Sulgrave that this name was not an invention but was how the island was named on British charts. There was a barber, a smiling man with a distinctly oriental face, and several women who did laundry for the men on the base who could afford the luxury. "Mr. Sung," Dolfus said, referring to the barber, "is a Surinam Chinese. They're the Jews of the Antilles. The doctors, the dentists, the intellectuals. Superior people, sharpened by adversity." He looked at Sulgrave, observed, "Nobody wants them, because nobody can survive without them."

There was something about Dolfus which Sulgrave found intensely distracting. For one thing the man never seemed to stop thinking—brooding would be a better word for it. The nickname given him by his men precisely suited the cast of his face. It wasn't that he was thin or that he looked like a skull, but rather that there was a hollow-eyed nakedness to the face, an admonition against vanity. He looked as though he had brooded long on the riddle of his own mortality, and had found no answer worth attention. Yet there was a smiling quality to the face, even in repose: white wrinkles about the corners of the eyes stood out sharply against the deeply tanned cheeks; and the corners of his mouth turned up now and then as though bewitched by something, a private thought, a joke, something not quite funny but which threatened at any moment to turn funny. When he did smile, he managed to do it privately; that is, he didn't share his pleasure, but turned his face away almost as though embarrassed.

The Officers' Club was a joke, of course. Except for the beach, which was white and gradual to the water, there was nothing in the way of décor. The "bar" consisted of a single ancient kerosene-fired refrigerator that kept beer admirably cold, even though it smoked ominously and had to be cleaned once a day of soot. Dolfus opened two cans of beer and removed his hat. At precisely that moment the sun broke through the rain and vanished again. The rain started to diminish. Dolfus looked up, shrugged. "Three days of this," he said. He was not complaining, simply reporting a fact. Sulgrave nodded, uncertain.

They sat under the canopy of plaited palm branches and watched the tiny roll of surf that curled the lake-like edge of the lagoon before them. Then Dolfus said, with weary seriousness, "You're going to be his aide. You'll have to know what you're in for, what you're going to have to learn."

"I see."

"This island," Dolfus said disgustedly, "or, rather, *that rock*, was uninhabitable when we came here. Nelson once used it as a supply base, even had it commissioned as H.M.S. Manacle Cay so that he would have unequivocal command over it as a ship of the line. Now we've turned it into a rat's nest of tunnels and bunkers and are stuffing it full of ammunition. It's an unsinkable ammunition ship."

"Do you think the United States will be in the war?"

Dolfus laughed that curious private laugh, averted his face behind his hand. Then he said, "The Commander doesn't think so. He's convinced that the President is personally responsible for his being here. According to him, he's being punished."

"Punished?"

"He ran a tin can aground off Oahu. The next time he's drunk, you'll hear all about it."

"He drinks?"

"He drinks."

"I see."

"I don't think you see at all. Understand me, Sulgrave, if I didn't like him I wouldn't take the trouble to brief you. One of your jobs will be to keep him away from my men when he's drunk. He has an obsession about blacks, and I'm afraid that one of these days he's going to say something that's going to get him killed."

Sulgrave nodded.

"There's a lot of tension here, as you know. Otherwise you wouldn't have been sent down. I have my job to do—which is to carve out about two more miles of tunnels and ventilation spaces—and I have the men to do it. These men are good and these men are black."

"Construction battalion?"

"Part of one, yes. The rest of the outfit is building airstrips around the Lesser Antilles. I also have some Special Battalion troops for stevedoring and ammunition handling. I was hoping they'd send an experienced ordnance man down, or at the very least an old-time gunnery man."

"Something wrong?"

"Yes. They sent you. But I'll get used to the navy someday. Don't worry about it. That's the way it always happens, I suppose. The river boat comes up the Yangtze, the new arrival disembarks, portmanteau in hand, is met by the Old China Hand. Who invariably says, 'I somehow expected they'd send an older man.'" Dolfus sighed. "However, I guess it's the Old China Hand who has aged without knowing it. I'll get used to it."

To their left, out of sight behind a cluster of shacks, a child had started wailing, screaming actually—a small girl's voice that was full of fear and pain; she kept screaming, "No no no no no no . . ." Sulgrave noticed that Dolfus was alive to the sound from the beginning, though his awareness showed only

17

in a tiny frown, a frown almost of distraction rather than ir-ritation.

Dolfus continued, "This rock may be unsinkable, but it's not indestructible."

"Do you have special hazards in handling and loading?"

"We have a special hazard—Bonuso Severn Hake, who, unless I miss my guess, is overpowered by his conscience to the point where he despises himself. Makes him dangerous. I *do* care if he kills himself. . . ." He said it as though he'd been accused of not caring. "But I'll be damned if I see the justice of taking a bunch of black innocents down with him."

"I don't see what you're driving at."

"Don't worry about it then. When you see how much TNT we've got stowed here you'll see what I mean. This is an experiment in folly—but then war's folly too, so it cancels out, I guess. This island is expendable—understand that. Even the dumbest lout among my men knows that this place could go up any day, probably *will* go up someday—and not just from enemy action either. You may as well base your life here on the idea of doom—at least until you're out of here alive."

"You sound pessimistic."

Dolfus nodded, looked wise. Then he smiled. "Old Mithra-dates, he died old."

"You don't believe we'll be in the war, either?"

"No," Dolfus said. "But that has nothing to do with it. I believe that there will be war, and that we'll lose it. I believe that with this war we are witnessing the beginning of the end. But who cares?"

"I see," Sulgrave said. "What are you doing in the navy?"

"What I've always done. I'm hiding."

By midafternoon the restless sun was out, the sky was clearing, and Sulgrave could see for the first time the unbelievable tropical green that softened the black seaward rocks of Manacle Shoal. It was as though the rain had awakened these islands from sleep. The beach steamed in the drying sun; the wind was still.

It wasn't for several weeks that Sulgrave learned that Dolfus had held several choice teaching posts, was in fact a Rhodes Scholar, and that his long-term enlistment in the navy had been an act of intellectual defiance of a sort that Sulgrave would never come to understand. For Dolfus, as it turned out, believed in Armageddon; the end of his world was, to his mind, clearly at hand.

One thing remained in Sulgrave's mind from that first afternoon. One small incident. It set the eerie tone of his entrance into hell: the unseen crying child whom Dolfus ignored at first screamed again from time to time; finally, in what seemed a rage of exasperation, Dolfus arose, set down his beer and stalked off toward the shacks. When after twenty minutes he still hadn't returned, Sulgrave, feeling very much the outsider, wandered over to the shacks. What he saw was Dolfus in full-running, red-faced argument with an old fat native woman wearing laceless brogans who still held a switch in her hand. The beaten child was nowhere to be seen. But lurking behind Dolfus was another older girl of about fourteen, a beautiful child-woman; she was the first to see Sulgrave approaching and clucked a warning. Dolfus switched from patois to common English, and as he tried to end the conversation—the old woman unwilling—the young beauty tugged at his sleeve. Distracted, he turned to listen to something whispered in his ear—Sulgrave knew it concerned him—that ended in a low suggestive snigger and a copulative movement of the hips, an astounding gesture for a child. Dolfus turned angrily on the girl and the old woman cackled with a kind of self-righteous amusement. Dolfus walked away from them, rejoined Sulgrave.

As they walked back to the shade of the club, Dolfus was glum. "You'll know all about this place sooner or later. The old witch is called Mother-in-Trouble. You wouldn't think that a lovely thing like her could come out of that, would you."

"She's the girl's mother?"

"She's insane, of course, beats Girlchild for no reason at all. I still can't get used to the way people . . ."

"Girlchild?"

"You didn't see her. Actually, her name's Gretchen, but it became Girlchild in the mouths of these people. Girlchild is not hers—it's her niece."

"And the older girl?"

Dolfus said nothing for a long moment as he opened two more beers. Then, "Her name is Arielle, and she delivers the laundry to the base. Mother-in-Trouble is a laundress. They came here a few months ago—they're all temporary. This place used to be nearly uninhabited. Camp followers, I suppose you say. Working for the Yankee dollar, God damn it."

"Where did she get a name like that?"

"Arielle? Gretchen? Both are childed by the same father. He lived with the two sisters, I'm told. Was a Spaniard. Named Cintas. Loved Shakespeare, among other things."

"She's very beautiful."

Dolfus shot Sulgrave a glance. "Leave her alone," he said. "And keep in mind she's privileged here."

She lay for a long time. Naked. Pillow over her face in quiet exhaustion. No longer crying, she yet continued in the long helpless dream, recurring more and more often in recent years, which, since his death, had almost assumed the proportions of obsession. *Always remember, young woman, that you will be punished for being beautiful.* Why should that phrase keep coming back now, of all times? The old man had hated Bonuso Hake from the moment he set eyes on him, Annapolis man or not, hated him as only one rival can hate another; it was at the wedding—she didn't know until an hour before the ceremony if the old man would consent to give her away, so she had an uncle in the wings just in case—it was at the wedding when it all became clear and the old man, her father, half-drunk, half in tears, had said it. *Always remember . . . you will be punished . . .*

And so she had, as though the prophecy were self-fulfilling. The marriage lived with a curse on it, a father's curse; even though now they both were dead, they both still contended for memorial passion. At a level of thought she never would have noticed save for repetition, she knew that her father was still entangled in her most private and erotic thoughts and desires of and for her husband. When making love, either in reality in the past or in the present in the imagination, the image of her father obtruded itself and spoiled love, smothered it in guilt and unbearable shame. Somewhere in the corner of the room, more frequently now than in the past, was her father. He never watched her, but he was there.

The scene was always the same, only backwards. In real life he had searched her dresser and purses first, then, afterward, having found nothing incriminating, made her take down her tomboy pants and submit to being beaten—it was that much more than a spanking. And then, in absolute confusion and shame, as though coming to himself suddenly, he dropped her on the bed and withdrew from her room. She was left alone, utterly astounded at the emotions that coursed through her body like manic blood—she didn't hate him; she loved him. She knew she should be punished and so was ashamed of what she felt, and understood, therefore, why he had left her so suddenly. It was as though—no! not *as though* —it was: he had caught himself in the commission of an act of pure lust, was ashamed also. But in the fantasy, the sequence was reversed. First the beating, then the image of him standing furiously in the corner of the room searching her purses. Dumping things out, rooting hog-snouted through her private belongings, searching for one small lipstick which she'd hidden under her pillow. It was like a rape the way he invaded her privacy, and yet he was her father after all. He loved her and was trying to make her live up to something—it all had to do, she understood even at sixteen, with her mother, who had died quietly and without to-do a month before. Her father was lonely, and he had loved her.

It was the only time in his whole upright life that he laid a violent hand on her, and so strong was that scene printed in her mind that even now, at thirty-eight, and widowed, she could conjure it up in her memory and shiver with—with what? Fear? Delight? Shame? Yet she never knew clearly enough what it meant. She never told her husband, and to his dying hour he was ignorant of why she could forgive so

22

gracefully his rages, or why, to his even greater bafflement, she could so skillfully provoke them.

Vanna Hake hardly knew herself, so close to reflex instinct were her most intimate actions. And yet she knew finally. And it was in her letters.

Against mounting irritation that was almost hysterical, Sulgrave had searched the wreckage for some sign of life, but there was none. Something inside him revolted against the colossal insult of death—he'd never seen a dead man before—and evoked a rage that had no palpable object. It seemed crucially important that *something* be alive. But the men had been gathered for noon chow. There had been no place to hide.

Leaving Big Randy in charge of the other prisoners, he half-ran, half-walked to the eastern end of the island. The flat-bottomed scow was gone, but Skully's spare jeep was still there, parked in the lee of the rock behind the narrow strip of sand where the boat usually nuzzled. He hailed across the narrow cut, got no answer. Silence. Someone must have taken the scow. The only shacks he could see on Little Misery were wrecked, half-flattened by the shock wave that must have found its way around the eastern hump of the protecting rock. The trees across the cut were stripped of leaves in places, but they weren't charred and blackened as they were around the operations area on the Rock itself. Then to the southeast he saw a sail, a native sloop—that was why it was so quiet: they were gone, all of them. They had evacuated themselves. They would have used the scow to pile their belongings into, the sloop probably towing it.

Slowly, with infinite regret, he came to the conclusion that he was alone. It was Dolfus he'd really been looking for, on the slim chance that he had been with Arielle. But no, Dolfus was dead; Arielle was gone. In the wink of an eye, a whole intricate world had vanished. All the vanities, the involuted sorrows, the petty quarrels; of merchants, laundresses, lovers—all these had been wiped off the slate with a single turn of the wrist. For the first time since emerging from the providential tomb with the six other survivors, he wondered what small slip had caused the blast.

One other thing he wanted to do that afternoon, but didn't do, was to climb up and see if Dolfus' "Laughing Boy," the immense stone sculpture he had made, was still intact. Instead, he returned to the operations area with the spare undamaged jeep.

"We found most all of the Commander, Mister Sulgrave," Lace said. "Randy's lookin' for some dress whites to put him in. He was covered with dirt and blood, so we thought we'd wash him up a little."

"No sign of Lieutenant Dolfus?"

"Naw suh, Skully gone clean. Old Skully once tole me that when he gone he don't plan to leave no mess, and, man, he gone clean."

"He was a man of his word, wasn't he." Sulgrave knew he couldn't hide the edginess in his voice or the tears in his eyes, so he didn't try.

Lace turned his lean face skyward, shook his head ever so slightly. "He was a man, that for sure."

"The civilians seem to have left Little Misery."

"That's all right, too, now," Lace said. "They had their share."

Sulgrave knew that Lace wanted to ask about Arielle, but couldn't bring himself to break the taboo—all along, the men had carried on as though they knew nothing of Dolfus and the girl, out of respect for his privacy, Sulgrave suspected.

Sulgrave said simply, "The girl must be all right. The sloop's gone off. There was no fire over there."

Lace nodded without a word, went to join the others.

It was from the same ruptured sea chest where Randy rummaged up the dress whites that Sulgrave took the red leather box marked LETTERS FROM VANNA. In the lid was a picture of the dead Commander's wife; she lived up to Dolfus' exaggerations of her beauty. Even in a photograph she was clearly a striking woman. Without a thought of what he was doing, Sulgrave made a space in the wreckage of the Commander's little house and sat down cross-legged in what had been the bedroom, and began to read.

She wrote in a fine, controlled hand that utterly belied the eye-jolting references to her carnal fantasies. Letter after letter was salted down with loving and erotically explicit threats of betrayal; these were counterpointed with detailed four-lettered descriptions of her fantasy plans for her husband when he next arrived home. Guiltily he picked up the leather box and went to supervise the closing of the Commander's makeshift coffin. To Sulgrave, the sudden thought that she, of course, was still alive came like a flash of embarrassment.

She turned and looked at Sulgrave in profile. He was looking straight ahead, unconcerned for anyone but himself, she thought. It was an attractive fault in a young man. There was something odd in his manner, something not altogether proper to the occasion.

Closed car at four. Only it's not four.

At naval funerals the last come first I remember. Symbolizes equality in death, but I'll hold on to this boy. Where I go he goes.

"It is difficult for me to realize that I'm a widow," she said.

Sulgrave looked at her, uncertain.

"It's exactly as though I were on my way to my wedding," she said. "I remember I felt the same way. Edgy. It's really very good of you to be our best man. Death and I both thank you."

The edge of hysteria in her voice genuinely alarmed Sulgrave. Very sharply he said, "Stop it, Vanna," calculating that the abrupt use of her first name would act on her like a slap to bring her back to reality. It was the most he dared do.

He was right. She turned and gazed at him in something between amazement and bemusement. "How did you know that I was called Vanna?"

"I hope you are not offended at my use of your first name."

"Oh, but *not* my first name. My nickname." Some urge to keep the upper hand caused her to say, "And if you really wish to call me something other than Mrs. Hake, Mr. Sulgrave, I suggest you use Vannessa, which is my given name."

He had a choice: apologize for impudence or brazen it out. "My given name is Everett, which I have not liked since I was a child. I go by my middle name, which as you already know is Turner."

But she kept the advantage: "Yes," she said. "Lieutenant Dolfus mentioned you in one of his letters."

Silenced, Sulgrave smiled politely and gazed out of the window, remembered suddenly Skully's extravagant praise of her beauty; but never had he given the slightest clue that he had ever written her. Sulgrave digested the incomprehensible. It *was* possible: *Dolfus and her.* It suddenly made her more desirable, he realized, unable to think further for the shifting movement of his thoughts.

There was more beneath the cold-mannered beauty of this woman than Sulgrave wanted to know; her letters to her husband had come too close to overt expression of an explosive soul, and he knew that she must be lost in the flood of an immense change in her life—as though the bitterness of having kept herself secret all the years with and without her husband was just now coming to a head, like a blister that appears only after the long walk is over.

Irrelevantly, Sulgrave thought, she said, "I am sick of being cheated out of my life."

Sulgrave is thinking ahead, of the coffin, running over in his mind what Orval had told him. There is certainly no sense in making an embarrassment of the situation now. For one thing, he knows he has no choice.

I'll never know why. I'll never know why. Except that his being dead made his possessions also dead—I've expressed it badly, but that was it. Her letters were merely a part of him, at least that's how I felt *then*. If I had had a space of time or distance to think it over, I would have undoubtedly seen it differently, but as it was there was no time and I was marooned—I fully expected to starve to death on that island. Was I to know that the blast had broken windows a hundred miles away?

I'm lying, of course. I knew full well that his wife was living. I knew when I read the letters that I would someday meet her. I knew this both ways, spiritually and carnally. I read those letters because Dolfus had told me she was beautiful. I like beautiful women.

Why then should I submit to this self-examination? There is no reason for it, since no one will ever know unless I tell them. I won't tell them.

■

Like Ahab's boat crew, they showed up for the funeral. Even Ishmael couldn't have been more startled by their presence. They were under armed guard, of course, and very proud of their status. Being black, they stood out.

Big Randy looked much older, and who was to argue that he hadn't been through hell?

Vannessa Lee Lynch Hake, misunderstanding, thinking that the coffin contained only her husband, said, "They must have loved him."

Why argue?

There is something about the imminence of death that makes a man seek life in its most elemental and compelling forms; Benjamin Dolfus lived in what to him was the quiet foreknowledge of doom, and lived therefore like a being quietly enraged, afraid of nothing mortal. To a man less attuned to the dead certainties of mortal error, to a man like Sulgrave, younger in years and in experience, the risks of life were statistical; but to Dolfus, a man living with life, they were absolute, certain. He was a man cursed with the crippling gift toward prophecy. Yet crippled as he was, he got around.

Sulgrave's first meeting with Dolfus had been confusing and uncertain. He sensed in the older man a kind of intensity that he had never associated with a career naval officer; Dolfus was more like the pedestrian image of the brooding poet, except that there was nothing delicate in his person or appearance to support the hackneyed image. It took longer than an afternoon of drinking beer to know the man, the being beneath the image. When Dolfus left Sulgrave before the Commander's quarters that first afternoon, Dolfus left with his secrets intact. Sulgrave was unnerved.

In all the time he knew him, Sulgrave never heard Dolfus make any really essential reference to his prior life—he learned little of his prior service experience, of his life before joining the navy, almost nothing. Dolfus had had a wife, whom he referred to only once and then in the past tense—whether she was divorced from him or separated, Sulgrave never learned. Once the Commander in a fit of irritation referred to him as "that academic bastard Dolfus." That was a clue. But Dolfus, when questioned, amusedly admitted his birth, would go no further in discussion of the past. He seemed like a man without a past, or rather a man who addressed himself not to the past or future but simply to the present; he would often halt in mid-stride to gaze at some tree or stone or play of light that would have eluded Sulgrave had not Dolfus then shown it to him.

The relationship between Dolfus and Sulgrave cautiously settled into something like a tutelage or apprenticeship; Dolfus often asked him to join him for a walk or a "sit," as he called the long silent periods when together they would sit with beer cans warming in their hands and watch the sun squat into the purple sea. He always would ask Sulgrave to join him as though he were granting a junior officer a favor, or more exactly, a privilege; Sulgrave felt this order in their relationship; yet despite youth and vanity, both of which Dolfus made him sensible of, was always flattered when the casual invitation was proffered.

Moreover, in some obscure but important way, Dolfus seemed conscious of being a teacher. That was when things were going well. When things were going badly, Dolfus walked about the operations area silent and uncommunicative, as though burdened under the knowledge of his fragile and passionate mortality. At such times he wore his pessimism like a hair shirt but treated his men with extra love and respect, and indeed seemed to have some blind dedication to their special peace and contentment. They worked for him like slaves, a fact which only seemed to irritate Dolfus in a way so obscure that Sulgrave could never fathom it.

Dolfus' relation to his men was crucial to him. He fretted over them, goaded them when they were slow, listened to their troubles when they had them, settled their disputes, punished them, pardoned them, and called every one of them, not only by their first names or last, but by the curious and colorful symbolic names that they evolved among themselves.

He never let himself forget for an instant that his men were black; Sulgrave remembered when the Commander once jokingly called Dolfus a "nigger lover," Dolfus' head had jerked back for an instant, as though struck. Then he paused, cooled it, looked out to sea, and said, "Yes, I am a nigger lover." He nodded to himself. "Yes." That sudden ugly turn had taken Sulgrave by surprise, since the Commander's prior mood had been one of relaxed banter after a hard day's work.

Sulgrave later asked Dolfus what was behind it.

Dolfus looked at him. "The only way to learn to love yourself is to learn to love the whole world." He paused, evasive, looked down at the beer can in his hand, rubbing it with his thumb. "The meek shall inherit the earth." Then he laughed, turned his head away. The laugh was hollow, full of self-reproach and melancholy. Sulgrave had learned that this laugh signaled the end of a conversation, and said nothing more on the subject. Together they watched the sun go down. Not much later, the moon rose red out of the sea behind them.

Bonuso Hake was a violent man who didn't know it, and that made his difference. What there was of him to know was difficult for a subordinate to appraise, what lay hidden below impossible to guess. Indeed, were it not for one small thing, an appetite too awkward to conceal, he would have passed for the coolest man on the Rock. But Bonuso Hake, Commander Meander as the signifying Negroes called him, Admiral God as Dolfus called him—Bonuso Hake liked alcohol. He liked it only on occasion, but in large and un-stoppered quantities. When he drank, he drank alone, or thought he did.

Three men besides Sulgrave came to know the full extent of the secret; Dolfus, who knew all along; Orval BlueEyes, who knew because he cooked and cleaned up; Fireman First Class Randolph Handy—Big Randy—because he knew everything and was big enough to handle anything. The rest of the men knew that the Commander got drunk—that much of the word got out—but none of them knew of the rages and the smashing of furniture, sounds which they took merely for aggravated revelry, since the phonograph played dance music at full volume during these eruptions. Also, the Commander could clearly be heard laughing from time to time, loudly and at length. Of course, they weren't seeing his face.

The Commander's quarters were austere, a simple frame bungalow, painted white against the sun, that nested slightly up the slope from the other buildings. The cleavage that made the operations area the only habitable part of the Rock sloped down to the water in a small open bight that made a natural deepwater anchorage; the whole effect was of a huge green amphitheater with a sparkling blue stage. The Commander's house was fifth-row center, with the rest of the operations buildings, barracks, workshops, mess hall, chapel, all crowding the orchestra pit. Since the audience faced west, mornings were cool until ten o'clock, afternoons blazing hot till six. And though the Trades blew unceasingly up the back of the Rock and spilled over the top out to sea, the waters of the anchorage under the wind's spillway were by day ruffled only by vagrant catspaws; from noon the men on the base worked in nearly still air beneath the overriding torrent of the Trades, men parched behind a waterfall, until nightfall when the Trades slowed and descended and cleaved once more to the leeward profile of Manacle Shoal Rock. Sometimes at night, or in the dark hours of the morning, the wind would carry the sound of Dolfus' solitary jackhammer from the far side of the island, and the men on dog watch would shake their heads. "Ol' Skully's makin' it again,"—or, "That man sure a rock choppin' mother,"— or again, "Don't the Lieutenant get enough of that rock ax during daylight, that he gotta go out whangin' away at night?" There were a thousand remarks, a thousand jokes, and in the beginning no one on the Rock knew why he was doing it. All he would say was, "I'm giving them something to wonder at, something to think about, ponder." Then he'd laugh and slide out of the subject, and in truth no one cared. It was something to provide comic relief, and when the night wind brought news of the distant puttering rock drill, the men, envisioning Skully wrestling with the drill and the awkward hissing air hose, would joke among themselves in the dark and, for some unaccountable reason, feel good.

But on occasion the wind brought other news—the sound of the Commander's phonograph—and no one felt good. As

35

far as the men were concerned, the white boss was getting drunk privately; the only consolation was that Dolfus, the only white man anyone gave a shit for, wasn't with him. Old Skully seemed to make a point of being duty officer whenever there was music up the hill. But the men knew also that when the Commander stopped juicing and came down, there'd be three or four days of hard times. For always following these bouts, there would be a redoubling of cleanup details, of barracks inspections, of policing grounds and painting rocks white, almost as though old Admiral God were making his penance public and his atonement a communal undertaking. At times like these the Commander would wander around the base poking his gloved finger into garbage cans, mattresses, tool cribs, "looking for trouble to make," as the boys in the gallery put it. And they gave him thus his name: Commander Meander. Till the day he died he never heard it.

But though the Commander could be a thoroughgoing stickler in matters of discipline, there was also in his nature a certain caprice that made his punishments unpredictable. Sometimes a minor infraction would earn a man a month in the empty bunker that served as the brig; on the other hand, it was not unusual for a serious violation—an attempted knifing or a barracks theft—to be dismissed with nothing more punitive than extra duty in the chow hall. A man caught through his own stupidity or carelessness was more likely to incur the Commander's wrath than a man tripped up by temperament or fate. And drunkenness, in the tradition of the "old navy," was nearly always a mitigating circumstance. Once, shortly after work on the base had begun (the tale, almost a legend, had been embellished in a hundred retellings by the time Sulgrave heard it), nine enlisted men from an earlier construction battalion now departed, had stolen a case of liquor from the hold of an anchored supply ship, and after ferrying a kidnaped jeep across to Little Misery, staged a midnight party that ended three hours later in a drunken figure-eight joyride among the shacks and coco trees of that scattered settlement. The eight men hung on the jeep (there *had* been nine, but one fell off and broke his arm, although he didn't know it till next morning) and careened back and forth past Mr. Sung's then new barber pole, changing drivers full tilt; the object was to see how close they could come on each pass without hitting it. But on the twenty-fourth pass someone's knee hit the light switch while changing places at the wheel, and they took the candy-striped pole with them. They almost took Mr. Sung in his nightshirt as well; the nimble barber leaped up into the house just in time. (But by his own account he wasn't so nimble coming out again; in the moonless darkness he couldn't have seen that the wooden steps were gone with the pole.)

The damage to the jeep had not been unnoticeable even in the dark, and must have exercised a sobering effect on the unauthorized occupants. For one thing, both headlights had been permanently extinguished and the windshield was cracked and crazed from the passing blow of the barber pole—it had sailed up over their heads and into the night behind them—and without a moon, seeing was difficult. More accurately, seeing was impossible. But the supreme logic of drunkenness had dictated that the vehicle be returned to the base, and all hands were turned toward the achievement of that miracle. The story came out at the inquiry afterwards. Walking abreast of the blinded jeep, they covered the ground to the cut in less than half an hour; only once did they stray into soft sand and have to heave the jeep back onto the beaten track. When they reached the cut, they lowered the ramp on the flat-bottomed ferry and drove the jeep aboard without mishap. That much was agreed on.

What happened next depended in its flamboyant details on which version one heard, but Sulgrave reduced the reducible facts to these: The stolen jeep was put aboard the ferry, the ramp was secured, the ferry pushed off and turned around. But it was several minutes before the outboard motor finally kicked over and started. The men had picked out a star that would take them across the narrow cut at right angles to the beach behind them, but they followed their star without being aware that a strong current was running and was carrying them sideways out to sea. A few men were said to have become concerned when the looming shape of the Rock occluded the guide star, but abandoned their uneasiness when a few moments later they felt the prow lift as it slid up solidly and grounded onto smooth sand. The kicker was stopped and, by the flare of a cigarette lighter, was covered with its tarpaulin in seamanlike fashion. The last of the bottle was reportedly passed around in congratulation and farewell before debarkation. When the ramp was lowered one man staggered out and got his shoes wet, came back, and climbed aboard the jeep. No one thought anything of it. Assuming that the extra weight in the ferry had caused the short grounding, the others logically followed his example and piled aboard the jeep to ride ashore. Anticipating that the overloaded jeep might bog down before reaching high hard ground, the driver put the machine in four-wheel drive and backed up in the ferry to get a good run. Then revving the engine to a high whine, he shouted *Here we go*, let out the clutch, and drove full-tilt across the narrow sandbar that defined the reef's entrance to the cut, into eight feet of water of the open bay.

Sulgrave learned that the source of the liquor was never

even officially inquired into. An inquiry had been held, of course, and all eight survivors (including the one with the broken arm, whom Mr. Sung had found sleeping beneath his house the next morning) were brought before Captain's Mast and given punishment. Yet, compared to the seriousness of the crime, the consequent punishments were light. The men forfeited pay and had to recover the jeep on their own time, were then remanded to the bunker for a short stay. But the serious part of the tragedy seemed to be blamed on the victim, the man who was driving the jeep as it plunged off the ramp. For he was drowned. In this instance the men agreed with their skipper; the Commander, it was said, had little respect and even less pity for a sailor who couldn't swim.

Looking back, Sulgrave could see that he'd known, long before he'd admitted it to himself, that disaster was certain. At first it was an impersonal realization, remote, impalpable, like Europe at war. But slowly it became part of his life to know that he was living in the shadow of irremediable death, that not only would the war spread from Europe to the rest of the world but that he, Sulgrave, was destined to help it spread. He understood vaguely that he was assisting at his own destruction, but it wasn't until Dolfus showed him death beneath his feet that he clearly understood. After that, he saw doom in the hollow of his hand.

As with everything Dolfus did, he did it indirectly. He asked Sulgrave if he would like to accompany him on an informal inspection of recently arrived munitions; they had been unloaded and stowed in unfinished bunkers and stacked under tarpaulins until new bunkers could be cut out. It was clear from Dolfus' remarks that he was apprehensive.

"They're crowding me," he said. "Getting in my way. They're trying to move in before the house is built."

"Isn't this bad practice?" Sulgrave asked.

Dolfus mused. "Bad practice? Depends on circumstances. They're sending the stuff down, so we have to put it some place. I guess there's no choice, would you say?"

"Couldn't they wait until you're further along?"

"Well, now. Before I came down here they showed me a British geologist's report that included this rock as one of the Limestone Caribbees. He was completely wrong. He made that report from an armchair, because if he had ever set foot here he would have seen that the coral is only an overlay."

"So it's taking longer than you thought."

"It's taking longer and it's tougher on our equipment. But we're holding fairly close to the original schedule. Washington wants a base? We give them a base." He fell silent. Then he halted in his stride and thoughtfully patted the nose of a three-inch shell that weighted down the tarpaulin of a waist-high stack of its mates. "Hello, buster," he said, as though patting a friendly dog.

"What does the Commander say?"

"Commander Bonuso Severn Hake is not happy with this assignment. He thinks it was given him as punishment for blundering onto that sand bar, and he's probably right. Therefore he is not about to complain that the rock here is too hard. He's not about to ask for a slowdown in shipments. His job is to build a stockpile of rocks for little boys to throw in case there's a street fight. But I'm afraid his Samson complex is getting out of hand. This isn't much of a temple, but it's all we got."

"But you think he's taking chances, is that it?"

"What would you say?"

40

Sulgrave looked around at the stacked munitions. "I'd say that no one had better drop anything until you get this stuff underground."

Dolfus smiled. "There's a whole boatload of torpedoes coming in tomorrow." He gave the tarpaulin a final smoothing pat, and turned and looked fully at Sulgrave. "You build bunkers on the theory that sooner or later there'll be an accident, and that at least the bunker will localize it. Nice theory."

"What will you do?"

Dolfus snorted. "What will I do? What will *you* do? We're both afflicted."

"What can I do?"

"You can do or die, that's what you can do. We're both living on the skinny edge of nowhere. Keep it in mind. As the diplomats are fond of saying, it's an explosive situation."

Sulgrave puzzled for some days over Dolfus' motives; except that Dolfus had sharply alerted him to the palpable reality of the danger, he seemed to have no wish to go further. He seemed to accept the possibility of disaster as a commonplace. In fact, he seemed easy with the idea that the island was doomed. At first Sulgrave had taken his references as jokes, jokes meant to ease the tension. Once Dolfus had settled an argument between two of his men with the comment, "It won't make any difference when we're gone, and we're all going. This rock will go sky-high tomorrow, so why argue?" The argument was halted. It was clear that Dolfus wasn't making a joke; he meant precisely what he said. It was slightly chilling to Sulgrave to realize that Dolfus had thought it all out carefully, rationally, and yet was able to accept the risk and live with it. It wasn't until much later that Sulgrave learned that Dolfus was living in acceptance of much more than mere risk: that the Rock would be destroyed

41

before any of them escaped was, for Dolfus, a fatalistic certainty, a quiet conviction. He conceived of his job as being to keep his men busy, reasonably happy, and to prevent their suffering over trifles. He saw them all as innocent, and doomed. That he himself would share their fate didn't seem to alter his compassions.

Dolfus' conviction of doom was, for Sulgrave, contagious. As he became more and more sharply attuned to the Commander's almost compulsive need to take shortcuts, entertain risks, and otherwise cut corners, it began to seem to Sulgrave too that sooner or later there was bound to be an accident. What was most curious, most ominous,.was that the only sane reason for hurrying the work along at such a heedless pace would be the imminence of war; but this was the one reason the Commander had no resort to. The Commander didn't believe in the imminence of war. He professed to see the European conflict as having no effect on American destinies, and he therefore was certain America would never enter the war. The grim lessons of the First World War, he argued, were still too much with the American people. And when Congress passed the Selective Service Act by only one vote, he was certain they would never pass a declaration of war.

It was not that the Commander didn't want war. He did. It was merely that, bitterly, he saw that the fates were conspiring against him to deprive him of a future. War would lead to a better command than the present one; therefore, since the Commander couldn't believe in a better future, neither could he believe in war.

His only vengeance for his present ignominy, his only penance for past error, would be to finish this useless idiotic task ahead of schedule. He saw risks in what he was doing; but the only real danger lay in failure. Above all, the job would be done.

There had been another time, another funeral. His older brother had been named Bruce Mifflin Sulgrave III, after his father and his father's father, and was already a sophomore at Harvard while Everett Turner (the family always called him Everett Turner from the day he revolted from the infant nickname Tarry, this a matter of some pride at the time, later at boarding school in retrospect a dubious victory; yet habit by then prevailed) was still encompassing the awkward mysteries of darkening body hair and changing voice. The day he learned of his older brother's death was a permanent snarl in his memory, a moment in time that would never come undone, a knot in a wet rope that slipped through the hands to a jarring stop, halted, and slipped on. What he did the day before he couldn't remember, nor what the day after. But of that day, particularly of that very shocking moment, he remembered every sight, every smell, every mood of light and shadow. The texture of that wintering afternoon was as clear as the rough feel of the back-yard tree he climbed after his mother told him the news. He climbed the tree to think, to study the fabric of his feelings—for he didn't like his brother really, or thought he didn't then—and it was there, in the crotch of a red maple, that he learned for the first time that jealousy is the scar of untended love. He was jealous of his older brother, the favorite, "the big cheese," who did what he pleased, but as he thought of the good times, of the times before Bruce had lost interest in him in favor of stupid girls, the scab of resentment cracked and fell away. And when he thought that it was Bruce who had even taught him to

43

climb this very tree, then it was too much. He sat swinging his legs in the dusk and falling leaves of late November and cried. He cried for lost love, for love embittered and thus wasted, and for a brother who might be watching him from somewhere in the sky but who would never again sit listening to kitchen sounds in the crotch of a red maple.

He had, he calculated later, been singing the *Te Deum*—they'd worked on it all afternoon in preparation for the Thanksgiving services—when the family was receiving the news. The choir would have to work even later because he had been cashiered as lead treble—Old Pussyfoot had tried him in the alto section but even there he'd croaked and piped on the *forte* hallelujahs. In the end he'd sassed the old tub of lard, and that was that. He was out altogether. As he walked home, kicking through the drifts of curbside leaves and smelling the sweet smoke of autumn, he worried whether the choirmaster would report the sassing incident to his mother, decided that he would omit that from the reasons for his dismissal. He walked home like a man fired from a job he'd many times wished to quit, finding that freedom too had its ambiguities. For one thing, it depended on how you came by it.

The moment he entered the house he knew that something was wrong.

For Thanksgiving they had the funeral to digest. Several aunts and cousins had stayed over to swell the ranks of the bleak feast and to offer what comfort they could with their helpless mortal presence. But the strongly missing son gave the family a dismembered soul, and the redolent turkey was stuffed with love and with tears. His mother had worked the morning on it, as was her habit, and had insisted that they carry on. Yet she was powerless to forget that her recipe

44

for turkey stuffing was the favorite of her favorite son. During dinner she faltered only once, when grace was said, but she caught herself and raised her chin, and his father caught the tiny movement and said, Perhaps you're right after all. And she said quietly, He's with us. From that strange moment, from the awesome weight of the silence that followed, Everett Turner never was beyond hoping that there was a God. And yet he hoped against hope, which seemed to him even then to make that hope important.

And now, no longer a child, he stood in a warrior's uniform, bareheaded before a warless warrior's grave, steadying the widow on his arm. It was unusual procedure, but it had been at her specific request that he stay with her. The light of the cold November sun was like the light of his brother's funeral and yet he was no closer to the mystery. The raw earth of the open grave was like a fresh insult, and someone had tried to cover it with a fantasy of grass; the brilliant carpet of artificial putting-green that covered the hump of dirt made a bitterly funny joke of nature, for nature's grass knew its season and was brown. The only other color was the flag, which was draped over the coffin with its blue field reversed, to be seen aright only by the corpse beneath it.

The senior officers had come last in the procession; the six black enlisted men, discreetly guarded, stood in the first rank by Hake's coffin, the last survivors of his last command, and mortal prisoners of his wrath. With bowed heads, white hats in hands, they listened as the prayers were given and then as one man rumbled a loud and real Amen. From behind them Amens answered, like echoes answering thunder, and then the first volley from the honor guard shivered the air. Three times their annunciation blasted skyward, a fierce and puny warning to any lurking evil who would invade the crucial open heart of the departing soul of the dead. Then, slowly, taps.

The procession left and rank was restored; the brass went first.

But none of this was what registered on the forefront of his mind. The impressions had merely worked in his gut to make him more aware of himself and of the flesh-and-blood woman who seemed to stumble on his arm even when she was standing motionless. The weight of her was live weight, and he was furtively aware of the softness of her and of the way she held him. She kept a grip on his arm that confirmed everything he secretly knew, that this was a fire in a palace of ice. Her face was utterly, even serenely, composed. She was precisely the widow, drained of feeling, submissive to her loss, bravely aware that life is short and man is mortal. Yet betraying this mask, her fingers, black-gloved and hidden, dug into his forearm again and again, as though in spasm. Once he even had to gently loose them out of sheer pain, and once he had to bear up her whole weight as her knees betrayed her. He couldn't tell whether she was aware of her state or totally lost in the private hell of her feelings. And yet, whether from fact or from guilty knowledge of her, Sulgrave sensed communication in her movements. Unconscious, perhaps, but not unknowing. She kneaded the flesh of his forearm as though lost in passion, as though driven by grief to heedless caress. And though everything told him that this woman was a woman whose grief was real, whose grief should not be profaned, still his thoughts rioted about a single image, some rare fire, the treasure that was in her. Dolfus had seen it, and had said it well: a woman of private beauty; in another age, a Helen.

Big Randy took his place beside the others and stood quietly through the prayers. When the prayers were over and the first volley was fired, Lace nudged him and said, "They gonna get us good."

"Keep talking they will, man."

"Don't you respect the dead, man?"

"A-men."

"Let 'em look inside that box just one good look . . ." Lace began.

BANG!

"Great God A-mighty," Randy breathed, "ain't you got no sense at all?"

BANG!

Taps.   Taps.

But Dolfus could talk when he had a mind to. He could provide an hour's or a night's entertainment, preaching or clowning, cursing or beseeching, chivvying or exhorting, or even just talking about nothing. He had a manner, a style for every mood, for every occasion. Every occasion, that is, that moved him to speech in the first place; there weren't many such occasions.

One night shortly after his arrival, Sulgrave listened from the shadows as Skully entertained the dog watch with an extended and erudite version of the labors of Hercules. Dolfus sat on the dock with a bollard for a throne and unspun the rambling myth as an old salt might have told a seaman's yarn. The five listening blacks leaned on the hose lockers and smoked—it was the only place on the dock where smoking was allowed, and then only when both ship berths were empty—and Sulgrave in his underwear watched them against the setting moon. Every so often one of the men would interrupt to query a detail or merely to comment, usually humorously, on some turn in the action. "What kind of ships did they use in them day?" And Skully would interrupt the narrative and discourse for a time on ancient ships and trade routes, on Phoenicians, on Crete, on lodestones and amber, on ancient means of celestial navigation, on the origins of modern customs (". . . you salute the quarterdeck because it used to be holy ground—they kept statues of their gods there"). After a while someone would ask what happened next to Hercules, and the narrative would resume until the next diversion. Sulgrave listened for nearly two hours—he hadn't been able to sleep and had come out to sit under the stars and relax. When Skully finally got up to go make his entries in the O.D.'s log he nearly stumbled over Sulgrave: "I was just going to wake you," he said. "It's your watch." Sulgrave said, "I was enjoying listening to you." Dolfus seemed embarrassed, even irritated at being over-heard. "I didn't know you were here," he said. He didn't add *otherwise I would have stopped*, but it was clear from his manner what he meant; Sulgrave had no business intruding on Dolfus' private relationship with his men. Sulgrave, to cover the moment, said, "You should have been a teacher." Skully relented, grunted, "I was." "What did you teach?" Dolfus said, "It was a long time ago." It wasn't until later, after he'd earned his spurs, so to speak, that Dolfus told him he'd even once been an instructor on a teaching fellowship in physics at Sulgrave's alma mater.

At first Dolfus had seemed uncertain of Sulgrave. While he didn't distrust him actually, it was clear that neither had he unbounded confidence in the younger officer, the newly arrived unknown quantity. Sulgrave's position as de facto adjutant to the Commander put Dolfus at one remove from Hake, a situation which he seemed to have desired and yet distrusted. It was clear from the beginning that there was some kind of profound friction between the Commander and his prime mover Dolfus—for that was what Dolfus was, the fountainhead of plans and action—and yet the nature of this friction was hidden from Sulgrave at first. He had called on the Commander, in accordance with good protocol, the first hour of the morning after his arrival, and it was made clear then that he was to function as a buffer between the Commander and the rest of the world. It was clear also that the Commander too had ambivalent feelings toward the new situation he was creating, almost as though it were a situation not of his voluntary creation but something in which he'd been forced to acquiesce. By Dolfus? By the area Commandant? Sulgrave couldn't have then said, but he knew that his presence was not wholeheartedly welcome.

If the first interview with Dolfus the day of his arrival had been unrevealing, the first brief meeting with Hake offered even fewer clues. The Commander met him in his shirtsleeves but slipped into his jacket, with its symbols of rank, before seating himself behind his desk. Yet he didn't bother to button the jacket. Sulgrave remained standing throughout the interview; there was no other chair in the room, which was the front room of the bungalow where the Commander also lived. Bookcases covered two walls, and behind him a table was scattered with open volumes. The Commander had his desk placed so that his back was to the bay, which gave the visitor, when standing, a clear view across the veranda of the limitless shifting glaze of morning sea. There was only a light wind and Sulgrave was sweating from the short climb up from the operations area.

After some pedestrian inquiries as to his training and prior experience, the Commander outlined Sulgrave's duties. Aside from the usual paper-shuffling routines, which Sulgrave knew and expected, the chief injunction laid upon the new aide was to "keep people away from me." The broad formalities quickly over, the Commander relaxed slightly and swiveled in his chair to gaze out the open window—one of the louvered shutters was not secured and he reached out irritatedly and hooked it back against the wall. "Damn it," he muttered, "that boy will have to learn."

The Commander's appearance surprised Sulgrave; while he had formed no conscious image of what he expected Hake to look like, nevertheless the man himself came as a surprise. Eyebrows. The black furry eyebrows would give him an angry look even when he smiled, which he hadn't yet. Black eyebrows were the unlooked-for, unexpected detail that instantly distinguished his uniqueness, particularly because of the contrast with his hair, which was also coarse, but wavy, and as gray as old lead tinsel. When he talked he looked at his visitor only in brief flashes, as though he knew that the pale, almost colorless intensity of his eyes had to be administered in small doses if people weren't to look away.

Sulgrave took advantage of the Commander's back being turned to lean discreetly forward over the desk to read the title of the battered and dog-eared book that lay with a paper knife in it for a place mark; it was Gibbon's *Decline and Fall of the Roman Empire*. The Commander laced his fingers behind his head and sighed as he stared away out to sea. Without turning around he asked, "How do you like our island, Mister Sulgrave?"

"Very well, sir. It's a beautiful place."

"Don't let the beauties of the place carry you away. I have been sent here to do a labor which you may have already decided is ridiculous. But whatever you think . . ."

"I don't think it's ridiculous, sir. When I was briefed in Washington—"

Hake swung around in his chair. "You say you *don't* think it's ridiculous, Mister Sulgrave?"

"No, sir."

Hake grunted. Irritation? Satisfaction? Sulgrave wondered what he was thinking. Hake swiveled back to the window; Sulgrave studied the back of his head; it offered no clue.

There was a silence. Somewhere in the hazy morning, a gasoline concrete mixer puttered an irregular jazzy rhythm.

"We *are* at war. With this rock," Hake said, stamping one foot unconsciously. "It is hard, unyielding, stubborn as hell.

It breaks tools, plays for time, fights back in a continuing delaying action. I'm behind schedule."

Sulgrave said nothing, waited.

"The men I have here are all Nigras"—Sulgrave noticed for the first time the Commander's ever-so-slight southern accent—"and while some of them are hard workers, a large majority of them are nothing but lazy surly unintelligent children who joined the naval service because they couldn't get anyone else to hire them. Do you understand me?"

"I'm not sure, sir."

"One of your jobs will be to ride herd on them. In the next room you'll find a surveyor's map of this island with the plan of work laid out on it. It's tacked on the wall. You'll take it down to your office when you leave here today. In addition to that there is a work schedule, which you will also remove with you, that will show you precisely how far behind we are on this job. We have adequate men and equipment already on this island to do the job. I don't want to hear any requests for more. We'll do this job with what we've got, is that clear?"

"Yes, sir."

"Some of the men here think I'm driving things too hard, but I'll drive a lot harder if we haven't made up the time we've lost within the next four weeks." He swung around in his chair and slapped his hand on the volume of Gibbon. *"This job will be done on time, Mister Sulgrave, even if I have to resort to courts-martial to do it.* Is that clear?"

"Yes, sir."

Hake's manner relaxed. "Tell me, why don't you think this enterprise is ridiculous?"

"Why, sir?" Sulgrave searched his mind for the reason behind the question before he answered.

"That's what I said. Why?"

"Well, sir, I should think that in the event of war, we'll need all the advanced submarine bases we can get. Especially on the approaches to the Panama Canal."

"Hmm. I see Mister Dolfus has given you his little talk about this being an unsinkable ammunition carrier."

"Well, sir . . ."

"Sulgrave, you're a green officer. You know that, don't you?"

"Yes, sir."

"Well, forget it. I want you to act as though you've been in the navy for twenty years. In your daily contacts with the men down there I want you to remember that you carry all the weight and authority of my office. Conduct yourself accordingly."

"Yes, sir."

"Tell me, do you think the United States will be going to war?"

"I don't know, sir."

"Come. A candid answer."

"It seems very likely, sir. I don't see how we can keep out, unless . . ."

Hake grunted again, as though he'd heard all the answer he wanted, and turned back to the window. "You're to take Lieutenant Dolfus' office. He will move into the dock master's shed as soon as it's finished. In the meantime you two can share space." He turned around and rose from his chair. He was smiling. Sulgrave was surprised to see that his whole face changed when he smiled, that, in fact, he was a handsome man, probably capable of great charm. The Commander came around the desk and held out his hand. "I hope you found your quarters comfortable, Lieutenant?"

"Yes, sir. I have a nice view of the bay."

"Good. Now if there is anything you want, don't hesi-

53

tate to call. I'll post a memorandum defining your functions so that you can hit the ground running."

"Thank you, sir. I was going to ask about that."

"I will expect you to come here each morning with the daily progress reports and the log. At ten, please. You will lunch with me from time to time and let it be known that you are doing so—it will help illuminate your status. And for the rest, I expect to see you each afternoon before the close of business, say, at five. I'm sure you have questions, but save them and ask me all at once tomorrow. It is my habit to nap in the early afternoon, and at such times I wish to be disturbed only in matters of urgent importance requiring my notice or decision."

"Very good, sir."

"One more thing, keep in mind that you are not in the chain of command. You are a staff officer. When you give directions always give them in my name. 'The Commander wishes so-and-so to be done.' Never give a command on your own if you can help it. Any decisions you make in my name I wish to be advised of in time to countermand them. Otherwise you will have reasonable latitude and discretion in the pursuit of your functions."

"I understand, sir."

Hake smiled again, and waved his hand toward the bookcases in the room. "You may avail yourself of my library any time you wish, Mister Sulgrave. Are you any relation to Captain Sulgrave who fought under Bainbridge?"

Sulgrave was taken by surprise. "I don't know, sir. Possibly. There aren't very many of us."

"Well, don't be too anxious to adduce the connection, Lieutenant. He was not a very distinguished hero. Committed suicide after losing an engagement. Not mentioned in most naval histories."

"Oh."

"Then I'll see you tomorrow morning at ten. You'll ask Lieutenant Dolfus to accompany you. You needn't come this afternoon. We'll start officially tomorrow."

"Thank you, sir. I could use the time today to get settled into my quarters."

The Commander shook hands, and Sulgrave noticed that he hadn't shaved yet that morning and that his eyes were red-rimmed from what could have been lack of sleep.

As Sulgrave went down the steps, the Commander said, "Remember. We're at war with damned black rock. Keep that in mind and don't let these men forget it. I don't like stowing material in the open, but until they get those tunnels cut out there'll be no other place to put it. And I don't want to hear any more suggestions that we slack up on shipments from the States. That's out."

"Yes, sir."

"It won't hurt to drum it into them. I think of it all the time, no reason why they shouldn't. Even when I'm asleep, I think about it. I dream of digging tunnels in black rock, Mister Sulgrave. Even when I'm asleep, do you understand? I want them to stop conspiring to break tools and waste time, I want them to get on with it. I'm the hand, Mister Sulgrave. From now on, you're the whip."

Hake smiled warmly, as though he'd cemented an alliance. They shook hands and Sulgrave took his leave. He walked down the hill at an easy trot; going downhill, it was less effort to jog than to walk.

was me   I was the wrong one
it was worse   his going away alive
At sea   liked the hiss in the word
                           how did he say it
at ssEEa   *I will die too*
when he was at sea it was worse   *empty*
and it wasn't just the waiting   *oh hold him*
   it was me   I was the wrong one

                                    sooner or later
   the waiting
   from the first   taught me to be
a widow   not a wife   *now him dead*
and now my his our son dead too
midshipman Hake   *his son's son*
                        floating full fathom with open eyes
unrecovered   *best he said   best   oh no*
                           oh ache to kiss those hurt
                     drowned eyes   hair black with seapitch
what month are we   *roll rolling*
it's bad this time of year   out in a sea
no small boat should be out in oh no small boat
should be out in   Looks bad if he's out there
         looks bad   sir   *always always*
                                    alone alone listen
Oh God what mind and memory make up love
I always hear behind my eyes that
belling buoy   oh God   *bone lonebone*
that plunging bell   *gang bong*

turning wild on that empty
tilting sea   *ganggone bong*
twisting   *gone   gone   longgone*
how did I know   I hear death
before I see it   I should have stayed
ashore   not seen that frail wreckage
Ben knew
   Oh God I hated you husband
   accident ha   *oh I sneer sneer*
Ben knew   *sneer despise spit on*
   he must have tied up to the buoy
   waiting
                                        swimming swimming away
Well   the sea made a man of him
   and you too   how do you like it
under your flag seadog   Ben never told
   knew   never would tell you in
a million years man to man   Except for
                                    lady you loved him
All right all right all right
   Jackass funerals
no don't drink   don't cry when the news
comes   news becomes   navy wife becomes
her husband's rank   is married a navy
widow
   at sea   waiting   with maybe him
already dead   I never really did know
did he know that   did he know what I kept
inside me all these deaf and dumb years
   They say you don't cry and I don't
I don't cry
                                    I hate I hate I hate

   No no don't let go

57

Hold onto his arm   they're all
watching you   I don't care   I'm not a
navy wife any more   I don't care
     No no   Breathe breathe   hold
     Stop
     Now think
     Think
     Think right
     I loved him really   was I waiting
for this all those times
and all his lovely words   words that sailed
instead of ships   moved in fleets around
the world   word commander
     The first thing is to burn his letters
they'll drive me crazy   navy wife navy widow
navy wife joke Schultz is dead
     Poor baffled lover   God woman think
     He was your husband   can't you feel
     I'll burn his letters
     said once he'd die with a needle
through his nose   a sailmaker's needle
                                        the sea is quiet
     God he must be a mess inside there
used to roll himself all over me

                                                            son killed him

     No think
     Keep thinking

                                                            he killed me

     No God no   get ahold of yourself
and now   and now   oh please please
     And now he's a box of garbage
Oh my God now they're going to bury him
                                        stuff his mouth with words

58

randy mare in springtime   image of lust
they won't bury the flag   it will stay
they'll hold onto it   slip it off   *God God*
   and him fooling that morning in
the kitchen   I was so proud of   our
first flat and my black enamel floors
penis erectus non discriminatus est or
something   they say in rigor mortis
   probably not true   *vigor mortis*
   oh God   wrong things to be thinking
but oh please please I want him again
   Like it was then   why do I feel
so wrong   *before before before*
   Oh God God   can't you see I'm going
oh no   don't tell me I'm going to faint
   oh no no no no no it can't happen
hang on him hang   hold me up   *hold me*
   Take a deep breath   *o hold me lift me*
   O Lord I can see the box now under that fairweather flag
           which way's the head   *the mouth the eyes*

59

Sulgrave left Vanna Hake in the care of another officer, an Annapolis classmate of the deceased whom he'd been introduced to but whose name slipped him, and approached the group of prisoners as they stood waiting for the van that would return them to prison. They'd been transferred temporarily to Washington for the investigation of the disaster, from whence they would be remanded to naval district headquarters for trial. Lace saw him coming and came to attention, alerting the other five; their conversation ceased.

Big Randy made a wary nod. "Afternoon, Lieutenant."

"Hello, Randy." Sulgrave returned the salute casually. "How did you boys manage this?"

Lace took it up. "Well, sir, he *was* The Man"—he said it with capitals—"and he probably wasn't such a bad stud if we'd got to know him. An' we all thought it would be nice to do right by his memory, an' so here we . . ."

Big Randy almost sneered at Lace, a gesture of impatience. "You can stop playin' Uncle Tom, man. He know what's in that box, you outa your head?"

Sulgrave said nothing. Randy calmed quickly, looked furtively toward the guards, who had moved discreetly out of earshot. Then he said, "The Lieutenant didn't get us in this mess. Ain't no point Tommin' *him*." The others seemed to agree by their silence.

Randy faced Sulgrave. "No, sir. We got a lawyer. He fixed it for us to come to the funeral."

Sulgrave couldn't help glancing toward the guards himself, an unconscious glance that seemed to make him part of the conspiracy. He said, "You have to be careful of what you tell me, Randy. I will probably be called to testify against you."

Poke said quickly, "We wanted to come, Lieutenant. Only we couldn't a done it without help from him. He just got us permission, him an' the chaplain."

"Nice stud for a preacher," Lace remarked.

"I just thought it would be fair to tell you," Sulgrave said, "that I'll be under oath and I'll have to answer truthfully."

Orval BlueEyes stared at his feet. "I sure feel bad about *him*," he said, nodding sideways without looking up. Involuntarily they all looked toward the burial place.

"Man," Lace said impatiently, "I told you a thousand times, we put all of him in there was to put. At least all we could find. Now why can't you be a reasonable cat and stash it?"

"Yeah, but . . ."

Randy cut off discussion with a quick grimace of irritation. "Leave it be, man, leave it *be*. You want to get us busted for worse than we got already?"

Sulgrave asked, almost as though against his better judgment, "I imagine you haven't told your lawyer about it."

Lace was agitated, "Yeah, damnfool Orval had to go and blow his nose on the eagle's sleeve. Good thing he didn't tell that preacher, or he probably woulda stopped the buryin' "

"What should we do if they ask us?" Orval asked, almost in a whimper.

"Ain't gonna ask, Hamfat. We on trial for mutiny, not . . . not . . ." Then in a hiss of contempt and indignation, "Man, stop comin' on like a handkerchief head. You not behind a mule now. You still talk like a Mississippi niggah."

"I am a Mississippi niggah. And I hold with the ol' Book when it come to buryin' a Christian, black or white."

"Well, you got it both ways," Lace said sullenly. "Think of them cats that was unloadin' on the dock—got buried in thin air. Ain't *nothin'* left o' them. Not even footprints."

"Yeah, baby."

"*Good-by*, so long, *fare-well for-ev-ver.*"

"'Nuff of this jazz."

Sulgrave intervened. "I have to leave. I suggest that you stop arguing about the past and think about the future. You're going to have to answer to a charge of mutiny, and unless you keep your heads . . ."

". . . we liable to lose them," Randy finished. "Lieutenant, I know you a man of sense. What should we do?"

"Stick together. Listen to what your lawyer tells you. Tell the truth."

"That's gonna be like pulling a plow with six mules. Ain't going to cut no straight furrow."

"That's your lawyer's job."

Randy shook his head dubiously.

At that moment the empty hearse started its engine, which served as a signal for departure. The decorous, soft-spoken knots of people began breaking apart and drifting toward the static procession of cars.

"Before you go, Lieutenant . . ." Randy hesitated. "The Commander . . . I mean, did anyone . . . ?" Deliberately, he left the question discreetly hanging and glanced significantly toward the grave. The others seemed to turn their attention away, as though not to intrude on a private matter; only Orval BlueEyes refused to disengage his interest.

Sulgrave took pains to be casual, imprecise. "As long as

they have a positive identification—ah, establish that a man is dead, that is, and not merely missing—as long as they have enough to be positive . . ."

"What are you tryin' to spit out, Lieutenant?"

Sulgrave hesitated, then said directly, "I saw the coffin sealed in San Juan. Under the circumstances there was very little else they could do. I signed a receipt for it. Nothing was said."

"That still don't make it right," Orval said.

Abruptly, Lace said, "Cool it, Lieutenant, here come the seagoin' fuzz—" At Sulgrave's puzzled glance, he added a nod in the direction behind the Lieutenant. "—The Man with the Power."

A warrant officer wearing sidearms approached from the prison van at the rear of the clearing line of cars, and saluted as Sulgrave turned around. "Sorry, Lieutenant, but I have orders to have these men back before colors are struck. You know how it is, sir."

The attendant seaman guards straightened up, moved closer.

"Of course." Sulgrave returned the salute. He turned back to the prisoners; they were all watching him for the expected change in manner, the reversion to strict officer-enlisted man protocol. He didn't disappoint them. "Good luck to you men," he said. "I'm sure that whatever happens, you'll be properly defended in a fair trial. Listen to your attorney and follow his advice, and remember to conduct yourselves at all times in a manner that reflects credit on you, otherwise you might prejudice your case. During the trial, pay attention and look smart. Things like that can influence the court's opinion of you and shade the verdict—justice is never a simple matter of black and white."

Silence. Lace smiled. "We'll have it both ways, Lieutenant." Then he stepped back as they prepared to leave, and saluted.

Sulgrave watched them as they walked away between the guards, then turned to where the last of the funeral guests were murmuring gloved good-bys to the widow. Vannessa Hake was standing among a small group of intimates that included the aged and resplendent Rear Admiral whom she had introduced to Sulgrave as her godfather, and was being splendidly composed as she received each momentary mourner with good-by (". . . so good of you to have come all that way for Severn . . ."). Except for these restrained exchanges, she was otherwise as impassive as a ballot box; the last of the stragglers filed loosely past, a nod each, a murmur each, and went to their cars. Finally, car doors clicked firmly shut, engines stirred, and the last seven-passenger limousines rolled decorously away, an expensive crunch of curving gravel toward the squat field-stone posts that marked the exit.

Two cars yet remained: one the Admiral's; the other had brought the widow.

The old Admiral, the godfather, asked, "Are you sure, Vannessa?"

Sulgrave waited at a measured distance.

"Uncle Bemis, you're a dear, but I do hope you understand. That's why I didn't want to receive at home."

"I suppose people *can* be a burden at times like this," he mused.

"It's just that they're reminders. I've no wish now but to be by myself. I'm going to hide for a few days in Washington. When I get back I'll be more like my old self again."

The old man sighed, resigned with dignity. "Well, you've always done things your own way, Vannessa. Only you can know what's best for yourself."

"I prefer to be by myself for a time." She paused. "I don't want to go back to the house tonight. I promise to call you from Washington, but there's no need to worry. I'll be with friends if I need them."

After the old Admiral had bussed his goddaughter several times, he admonished Sulgrave to see that she was properly entrained for Washington and that her baggage was taken care of. He fussed over her, and delayed his leave-taking further with more last-minute injunctions. Finally she kissed him good-by and started him toward his car; his driver snapped to and held the door. And he was off, waving through the rear window until the car disappeared through the stone gate.

"He's such a dear old fussbudget," Vanna said when he was gone. Slowly they walked toward the other car; the chauffeur started the engine and got out to hold the door.

As the car rolled out of the cemetery gate, Vannessa reached forward and closed the glass partition. Then she leaned back and took off her hat and veil. "I've saved you the fare back to Washington," she said. "You don't mind hitching a ride with me, do you?"

"You mean you're going there in *this?* What about your luggage?"

"I firmly intend to start a new life. The first thing I'm going to do is to buy some clothes suitable for a middle-aged widow."

Sulgrave said nothing; she was ahead of him.

She turned and looked at him. "Don't you want to drive in with me?"

He felt like asking her point-blank why she hadn't asked him before they got in the car, but she answered without being asked. "I was afraid you'd take me seriously about wanting to be alone and make up some irrevocable excuse, just to be polite."

"Don't you want to be alone?"

"Does anyone?" she asked. She turned away to the window, repeated the question. "Does anyone, ever?"

It wasn't long before Sulgrave realized that Lieutenant Dolfus had more than one pastime. Since they shared one of the lower bungalows, although each to the privacy of his own room, it was hard for Sulgrave not to notice that Dolfus often didn't come back to his quarters when he had the evening duty. Several times Sulgrave noticed that Skully had already finished breakfast in the chow hall before he got there; at first he assumed that Skully had merely risen early. But gradually it became clear that on these occasions he slept elsewhere than in his quarters, or so it seemed. And on weekends he disappeared entirely, leaving sometime after inspection on Saturday and not coming back until Monday morning. For Sulgrave, it was a mystery where he could be. Once he asked him where he vanished to, but Dolfus evaded the question with a vague reference to getting off by himself whenever he could—"and I like to sleep under the stars," he said.

It wasn't beyond imagining. Dolfus had a curious secretive side to his nature which Sulgrave had recognized from the first weeks on the island. Saturday nights he knew where Skully was because usually you could hear him—those were his regular nights for sculpting expeditions. The chatter of the jackhammer drifted over the ridge on the breeze from the east side of the island, but when the work stopped and the men brought the jeep back towing the air compressor, Skully was never with them. If they knew where he was they weren't saying. Once when Sulgrave was on duty, they came back—it was after two in the morning—and Sulgrave helped the boys secure the tools; he asked them where Lieutenant Dolfus was. One of them said, "We left him there sittin' smokin' a cigar and looking at his statue."

Skully always managed to have some beer for these outings—it was thus more than a simple honor to be invited—and it was obvious that the boys this night had enjoyed themselves. But there was something arcane about their laughter, about their horseplay among themselves, that made it seem to Sulgrave that he was an outsider. They seemed like a fraternity, at one with each other through the shared pleasures of secret ritual—all just a wee bit heightened by the beer. Sulgrave felt—he had to admit to himself—excluded, even lonely. It wasn't the first occasion; he'd heard them some nights coming back singing, laughing and pie-assing among themselves as they put the tools away. And lying in bed at times like this, or even just hearing the distant chattering of the jackhammer while trying to read a mystery, he felt the bare memory of the pangs of childhood, of being too young to build tree huts with his brother's friends. Or at least not being asked. The memory of hanging around with a new catcher's mitt, hoping they'd ask him—he'd learned the hard way not to ask; not playing was better than risking the clear rebuff. Sometimes he'd be asked if, after choosing up sides, they came out uneven; he learned to play right field with a catcher's mitt.

He'd been thinking a lot about his older brother recently, perhaps because for the first time in his life he had time to think about him. Simple accident was what the family had said; suicidal recklessness was what his aunt had whispered into the telephone, not knowing he was listening in the hall. The question bothered him, but it wasn't until the night before he was to go away to college that he asked his father point-blank. It *was* an accident, his father said, but probably suicidal—his brother had gotten into trouble with a girl and was afraid of being kicked out of school. It was a shocking revelation for the young Everett Turner, yet bittersweet; bitter, because he had a gently raised sixteen-year-old's concept of virtue and his brother; sweet, because it had been his father who told him, man to man, adult to adult, equal to equal. From that time on he thought of himself as a man, accepted as a man; the knowledge of his brother haunted him like a responsibility, something he would bear as an adult for the rest of his life. He was twenty-one before he slept with a woman.

Born on the Massachusetts coast, his childhood ambition was to be a naval architect. But by his sophomore year he had wandered into the mysteries of Shakespeare, and ended well as a Bachelor of Arts in English Literature, but not without his first love's having led him into the Naval Reserve Officers' Training Corps. After a miserable postgraduate year in a Boston advertising agency, he said good-by to Boylston Street and accepted an active commission as an ensign. A quick promotion to lieutenant, junior grade, had sparked an old interest. Now he was nursing his first ambition; when he finished his hitch he was going back to school, and, barring a war, he would someday be a naval architect. He having thus decided to dedicate his life to splendid ships, the navy, in all its bland and inscrutable logic, assigned him to a splendid island.

By now the novelty of arrival was wearing thin, and the days lagged. He'd invented enough routine to cover his duties, and filled the chinks with reading. But evenings were becoming harder to bridge, and Sunday yawned like a chasm. Several times a week he went over to Little Misery to drink beer, often on Dolfus' invitation. But when it came to the Saturday night event, Dolfus invited no one but his boys. And occasionally he had dined with the Commander (but otherwise Hake was a hermit). Once or twice he'd gone to the recreation hall to play ping-pong or shoot pool, but it was clear that Hake frowned on fraternization with the men, whether because they were enlisted men or whether because they were black enlisted men, Sulgrave wasn't sure. But he suspected the latter. Sulgrave was sure it was one of the things Hake held against Dolfus, though there seemed a touch of bitter envy at the ease of Dolfus' command of his men. Whatever the basis of the antagonism that bound Hake to Dolfus, it was clear that both men preferred to keep it private. Dolfus moved about the base with great discretion, and whether by accident or by design he and the Commander never met casually, but always and only on official business.

One thing that puzzled Sulgrave was Hake's preoccupation with his library, as he called it. He often read into the far hours of the night—sometimes the special gasoline generator that provided electricity for his quarters didn't sputter off until the hour before dawn—and whenever Sulgrave visited him his quarters were scattered with open books. Nearly all the volumes were closely annotated with cryptic notes in the margins, and often blossomed with slips of different-colored paper apparently marking cross-referenced passages. It was almost as though he were involved in some complex research, yet the typewriter was never uncovered and Sulgrave had never heard it being used. The one time Sulgrave had opened it to use it—to type a short notice for the bulletin board about not wasting water—he'd found the ribbon so desiccated as to be useless.

The books in Hake's quarters were of all sorts, and in the few times Sulgrave had dined with him he'd learned that the Commander could talk intelligently on all subjects, that is, when he wasn't absorbed in a book at the table. But on these occasions Hake seemed more interested in testing Sulgrave's opinions, particularly his opinions on great men in history and events that shaped them. And though generous with facts, he rarely owned to an opinion. In fact, taken altogether, the casual recluse existence and slack manner of dress in quarters contrasted so violently with his sword-bearing, white-gloved ceremonialism of the Saturday morning dress-white inspections, that Sulgrave was hard put to imagine them as extensions of the same man. In quarters, when reading, he wore heavy tortoise-rimmed glasses that gave him the intense, almost stooped look of a scholarly fanatic; the beetling black brows beetled even more with the glasses on and made more remarkable the pale, questing eyes. And yet on parade he stood tall and white and infallible, became even more forbiddingly resplendent as he walked slowly before the solemn ranks of rigid eyes-front, his own eyes narrowed to slits, seeing everything, unerringly finding fault. On these occasions he was the quintessential symbol of authority and discipline. Even his one official idiosyncrasy—the ceremonial Navy cutlass he wore with such address—only served to reinforce the stern impression he sought to create. Among the enlisted Negroes he had a hard reputation, and they nicknamed him Admiral God only partly for satire and mainly for fear of his cunning punishments. On inspection, even Sulgrave stepped wide of the Commander's wrath, bewildered less by the dazzling uniform than by the double image he had of the man inside it.

It was during one of these inspections, curiously enough, that Sulgrave unwittingly cemented a genuine friendship with Dolfus and thus won entry into the life of the island. Up to that time he had hardly suspected the existence of a social life, thus would never have imagined that he was being excluded from it. Beyond Skully's Saturday night "art class" (which was what he'd since learned the men called it)—beyond that event for the select few, there was only the recreation hall and the "juice locker" (which he'd learned from the same source was the enlisted men's name for the Officers' Club, the padlocked kerosene icebox on Little Misery).

That there was a more intricate life pulsing beneath the calloused skin of insular routine, seemed so improbable that it never occurred to him to wonder about its apparent absence.

The fire drill was a gesture absolutely characteristic of Hake. Sulgrave had finished checking the hectic progress of the Saturday morning clean-sweepdown, and, satisfied that the master-at-arms had everything under control, had gone to his quarters to shower and change into dress whites and to await the precisely prescribed minute when he would mount to the Commander's quarters and accompany him in his stately descent to the operations area. There they would be joined by Dolfus, who would report that all facilities and personnel were ready for inspection; then would commence the two-hour round in the dreary heat, through the chow hall, the machine shop, radio shack, the dispensary—through all the small hut-like temporary buildings that were but ludicrous parodies of their counterparts at Norfolk, at Boston, and at all the immense and complicated places where at that same moment the same rigorous ritual was being pursued. And on all the ships at sea—at least all those in the same time zone. The thought gave Sulgrave a moment's pause; Hake's inspections seemed less like comic opera when seen against annihilated space and time. It was then one navy, one ideal entity, one organism, and nothing so symbolized that oneness as the unvarying ritual of Saturday inspection. It was a day of trial and judgment and atonement, only half a day of rest, a stern Sabbath. At least at noon they would be done with it, if nothing went afoul.

Sulgrave checked his watch and wondered where Dolfus was. It was getting late, and he'd been still tinkering with a bulldozer when Sulgrave had left the motor-pool area. Suddenly, as if in answer, Dolfus' boondockers boomed on the bare boards of the veranda and he burst in covered with grime and dripping sweat. He stood a moment breathing hard, and let his sun-blind eyes adjust to the cool gloom of the bungalow.

"You better jack your ass up," Sulgrave said, glancing at his watch. "The Old Man should be just about ready to strap on his snickersnee by now."

"Him and his goddamned sword," Dolfus said, catching his breath. "He wants this island honeycombed, let him carve it out himself. How the hell can I catch up on a schedule when he insists on pissing away a whole half working day on these brass-assed inspections?"

Sulgrave was used to Dolfus' fulminations. Every Saturday it was the same. He grinned. "How can you have a whole half-day, Skully?"

"Learn some elementary Group Theory and find out, Rover Boy. Did my whites come back?"

"Mother-in-Trouble brought them herself. I hung them over your foot locker."

Dolfus looked at Sulgrave a moment longer. "You say the old woman brought them, not Arielle?"

"Not Arielle."

"Did she say anything?"

"She said she had trouble washing them, trouble ironing . . ."

"Nothing about Arielle, though," Dolfus stated imperatively.

73

"No."

Without another word, Dolfus went to change. He was running the shower when it came time for Sulgrave to start up to the Commander's. Skully would just have time to make it down, but he'd still be sweating when they got there.

The inspection was routine up to the point of the surprise fire drill. Sulgrave, in the press of the moment, could only assume that the Commander had hatched his plot the previous Saturday upon having noticed that the men, in dressing up the pier, had disconnected the fire hoses so that they could be more prettily coiled. Nothing had been said at the time, nothing thereafter. In fact Hake said nothing even to Sulgrave until they were walking down the path just prior to the start of inspection.

"I want a fire drill today, Mister Sulgrave."

"Yes, sir. I'll tell the petty officer on watch." He raised his clipboard, pencil poised. "At what time, sir?"

"You'll tell no one, Mister Sulgrave. If you tell one, you tell all of them. Those blacks have a grapevine that works in all seas and all weathers. We've never had a fire drill that they didn't know about in advance, almost before I had made up my own mind."

"Then you want me to have Lieutenant Dolfus . . ."

The Commander ignored Sulgrave, went on. "When we are halfway through the personnel inspection, you will wait until we reach the end of a rank and separate yourself from the inspection party, leaving your clipboard with Lieutenant Dolfus. You will then proceed inconspicuously to the pier, and without alerting the pier guard of your intention, will then sound the alarm. I will give permission to break ranks. After the drill, you will enlist Mister Dolfus' aid in re-forming the ranks, and we'll finish our inspection."

Sulgrave was incredulous. "A fire drill in the middle of inspection, sir?"

"Precisely, Mister Sulgrave." The Commander's tone was suddenly icy with reprimand. "You have captured my thought precisely."

Sulgrave snapped back to regulation protocol. "Aye, aye, sir!"

They walked the rest of the way in silence.

Dolfus joined them, and the inspection of facilities went quickly for once and without a hitch. But not once was Hake out of earshot, and Sulgrave had no choice but to contain the Commander's secret, although he mightily wished he could tip off Dolfus so someone could be planning ahead. Finally, resigned to it, he simply concerned himself with the inspection.

When they were halfway through the ramrod ranks of men, he excused himself and handed the clipboard to Dolfus. Dolfus looked quizzically at Sulgrave; the Commander said stiffly, "You have my leave, Mister Sulgrave." He walked away feeling Dolfus' eyes on his back, and feeling something like a betrayer. Dolfus would get the chewing-out if the fire drill was slower than standard.

As he passed the foot of the pier, the seaman guard saluted smartly and said, "Mornin', suh," in a rich Alabama roll. Sulgrave returned the salute and the greeting and walked around behind the master-at-arms' shack, where up a short ladder on a raised platform stood the hand-crank siren. He climbed up and stood for a moment, out of sight and alone, listening to the wave-lapped silence he was about to rupture. Then, feeling like a conspirator lighting a fuse to a bomb, he leaned his full weight into the slow-moving crank: first a rush of wind, then, as the handle slowly yielded under his weight, a low growl. The growl rose to a rising snarl, then to a steady, full-chested wail. One thought obscured all others: he was aghast at all the noise he was making.

Pushing the siren was hard work, and when he at last stepped back and let the handle coast he was sweating. Then he descended the ladder to the siren's dying wail, and turned the corner of the M.A.'s shack to await uneasily the results of his furtive errand.

In reconstructing later what happened, one thing was clear: that the men had nearly panicked. Dolfus himself felt partly responsible for this, because as he said, "They could see in my face that I wasn't expecting any drill." After the first astounded instant, Dolfus forgot all about the Commander and gave an order: "All right, you men know what each man's supposed to do and where he's supposed to be. Now let's get there!"

The Commander pressed a button on his stop watch and stood like a rock in the torrent of men that swirled past him, each man thinking of the tons of explosives that had passed through his hands from ships to the dock, from the dock to the rubber-tired dollies, from there to the bunkers and storage tunnels. Even more they thought of the tons of destruction for which there had been no room in underground storage, and which lay stacked under tarpaulins in the open near the dock. Each man ran toward his post wondering where hell would erupt; until the fire brigade got their equipment out no one knew where to imagine the fire.

Sulgrave went directly to the dock, and saw for the first time the disconnected hoses. The full extent of the panic wasn't clear to him then, and he turned back to rejoin the Commander without telling the pier guard that it was a drill. But before he covered twenty yards, he was met by the running shouting flood from the parade ground. For a moment, as he saw their faces, he was perplexed, then astonished; of

76

course it wouldn't occur to them that it was a drill! Who but a madman would schedule a fire drill during inspection? That was the one time when everything was put aside in dedication to the holy rites of spit and polish; nothing came before inspection, not even sick call. Sulgrave stopped one man, a squad leader with a coxswain's rating: "It's only a drill," Sulgrave shouted. "That's not what 'Tenant Skully says," and before Sulgrave could argue, he was out of his grasp and gone.

He was standing, wondering at the vague feeling of apprehension he felt, when the Commander came into view. He was walking slowly, alone. Dolfus would be off to the fire brigade.

The Commander must have seen worry in Sulgrave's face, for the first thing he said was, "It won't hurt them to feel a little urgency in these matters of fire prevention. I've noticed they've been getting careless lately. Perhaps this will cure it."

At the pier, the men worked with a kind of frantic relief: frantic because they knew they were at the mercy of chance should an explosion come elsewhere; relieved that the fire at least was not in their sector. The Commander stood with Sulgrave at the foot of the dock as the narrow, high-pressure hoses were snaked out and laid flat along the dock. Precious time was consumed as the hoses were turned onto their connecting standpipes; but worse, the close timing of the drill was thrown off. Each hose man had to first connect his hose and then run out the dock to the nozzle. From somewhere behind the M.A. shack the heavy chug of the sea-water pumps had already begun, and Sulgrave had only a split second to realize what might happen, when it happened:

The last man to get the wrench was still tightening his hose connection when someone at the pumphouse opened the valve that sent pressure to the dock standpipes. Since the

77

last hose man couldn't be in two places at once, the twenty-pound brass nozzle lay at the end of his hose untended. When the pressure hit, the hoses stiffened for an instant, then spurted, coughed, then full-streamed The last hose man dropped his wrench and ran for his nozzle, but it was too late.

Instantly two men were knocked flat by the wildly flailing hose, but they kept control of their hoses. Like a hissing serpent twisting in the throes of death, the hose rose writhing over the heads of the men, then slammed its nozzle onto the heavy planks. The whole dock boomed like a drum. Men were running out onto the dock, shouting, trying to help capture the runaway hose. Other hose men tried to edge backward out of the range of the flailing nozzle but the wild hose seemed to follow them; several were caught in the confused crossfire of high-velocity streams and went down in a slither of spray and water and twisting bodies. From the beginning, the Commander was shouting, "Close that valve! Get that damned valve closed!" Two men were frantically twisting the valve which would cut off the water at the foot of the dock, but chaos had already outrun their efforts.

Suddenly there were more shouts from the pier, shouts of real pain this time; the wild hose was standing over a felled tangle of men and whipping in slow fury at their huddled backs. Other hoses would soon be let loose if the men couldn't get clear of the demon pounding at them; it was suddenly clear to Sulgrave what had to be done.

In the full instant of necessity and revelation, Sulgrave turned without hesitation and had the Commander's cutlass out of its scabbard. Instantly perceiving his intent, the Commander nodded vigorously—"But be careful of it!" he shouted, as Sulgrave scuttled forward amid the tangle of hoses trying to pick out the one that ended in the untamed nozzle. Two enlisted men saw what he was doing and traced it from the standpipe, sliding it along in their hands as they ran toward him, bringing the dragon to St. George. There the three of them cleared a space and laid the hose down. Sulgrave went down on one knee, sword upraised, as the other two men prepared to restrain the hose after it was cut. Then the cutlass flashed down and the whole tableau vanished in a magnificent eruption of water.

The sudden geyser completely blinded Sulgrave and nearly knocked him off balance and he couldn't see to take a second whack; he couldn't find the hose, no less the cut he'd made in it. Feeling blindly he found the hands of the other two holding the hose and traced by feel to the cut. Then, eyes shut, unable to breathe for the blinding welter of salt water, he tried to saw the blade into the cut and nearly had it whipped out of his hand by the force of the blast. He tried several times before giving up for fear the blade might strike one of the other men; he knew they were next to him but he couldn't see them. One of them was shouting, "Hold 'im, man! Don't let loose!" Then, "How *you* doin', Lieutenant?" He opened his mouth to say Lousy, and was nearly drowned. He was sitting on his heels despairing of ever cutting the hose all the way through, when the force of the stream suddenly abated, the furious hissing softened to a whisper, and the fountain dwindled to a dribble in his hands. As he opened his eyes he felt the rock-hard hose soften and go limp—someone had finally closed the valve—but a heavy impenetrable curtain of water was still falling all around the three of them. For a split instant he was at a loss, until he grasped that this was the same water coming down that a suspended moment before had been geysering up.

That was the picture revealed to the astounded onlookers as the last of the geyser's great stage curtain fell about their feet, leaving the three drenched and dripping actors alone

79

and bewildered on a cleared stage. There was silence for a moment, and Sulgrave could still hear the hissing in his ears when laughter and cheers went up from the men at the foot of the dock.

Miraculously, no one had been seriously hurt, although several of the men nursed severe cuts and bruises from the drubbing they had taken. From weary, frustrated despair, Sulgrave's mood changed to secret elation when he found out that his first blow had been enough. The gash in the hose had relieved just enough pressure at the nozzle to bring it to earth; it had fallen as though exhausted, convulsing feebly until someone straddled it and brought it under control. Sulgrave rose to his feet and acknowledged the cheer with a weary ragtag wave of the sword. One of the two enlisted men who had helped him clasped his hands over his head and did a little sparring dance like a victorious boxer; the other one merely eyed the evil hose with suspicion, leaned down and examined the gash with his finger. "Lieutenant," he said, "this thing ain't dead yet—it only wounded." Sulgrave laughed and slapped him on the shoulder.

Dolfus had arrived in time to see the final action, but said nothing as Sulgrave came off the dock. White-faced with fury, he was giving orders for the cleaning up of the twisted shambles on the dock, when an enlisted man came up and handed him Sulgrave's water-logged hat. He passed the hat to Sulgrave, said, "Here's your hat"; nothing more. Sulgrave said, "I didn't know about it in time to tip you off, I swear it. He didn't tell me until we were coming down the hill." Dolfus looked narrowly at him, as though to see if he were telling the truth, then softened. "I should have known," he said. Then he added a wry smile. "Why didn't you bust his god-damned pig-sticker off at the hilt while you were at it?"

"Damned if I didn't try," Sulgrave said, shaking water off it.

"Mister Sulgrave, would you come here a moment?" It was the Commander.

"The Admiral wants his boarding iron back," Dolfus said. "Why don't you give it to him in the ribs?"

The Commander, who had also received a wetting, was standing with a group of petty officers as Sulgrave approached; he said, "I want you to find the man who left that main valve open and place him on report."

"That valve is usually left open, sir. To save time in an emergency. Also, if it were to freeze up or jam, it would be better for it to jam open."

"Then whom do you find responsible for that fiasco?"

"Ordinarily, each man is on his hose before the pump is started, sir. There should be valves at the standpipes, perhaps, but there aren't. The hoses were disconnected today for inspection."

"Is that how you explain that disgraceful performance?" It was the first time Sulgrave had ever seen Hake bluster, but he was perilously close to coming apart now. Dignity hung in the balance.

"It was an accident, sir. I'll see to having proper valving installed on the . . ."

"Mister Sulgrave"—the Commander was suddenly icily in control—"that was not an accident, it was stupidity. A man might have been killed. There is no room for accidents or excuses on this kind of operation. I'll have no accidents, and I'll have no *excuses*." The hated word was hissed through clenched teeth. "Is that clear?"

"Yes, sir."

"You may carry on, Mister Sulgrave." The Commander turned and walked away toward the path up the hill.

Unthinking, Sulgrave called out after him, "Shall I secure the inspection, sir?" The Commander ignored him, gave no answer. Sulgrave watched him walk away, and realized that he couldn't have asked a more tactless question. He felt he needed Dolfus, and turned about to find him. Only then did he realize that his hat felt soggy on his head, and that he had the Commander's ceremonial cutlass still in his hand.

They drove through the November landscape in silence for a time. Then suddenly Vanna said, "I didn't know those men were prisoners."

"Who told you?"

"Uncle Bemis. He was furious over their being there."

"Why?"

"He said they were mutineers. Is that true?"

"One of your husband's last official acts was to draw up specifications on a charge of mutiny and send it off."

"Are they guilty?"

"I suppose so. It didn't have to be a mutiny charge, though. I think that was a mistake."

"Oh, that bastard. He would never make it easier if he could make it worse. He wasn't always like that, you know."

Sulgrave said nothing.

"Did you like him?" she asked, after a moment.

"I think so," Sulgrave said, not hiding his uncertainty. "It's hard to know what you feel sometimes."

"I loved him," she said, grimly. "I loved him and was ambitious for him, but I failed him. At least that's what I used to think. Now I'm beginning to think he failed himself. That was Ben's theory all along."

"Ben?"

"Lieutenant Dolfus. He was a good friend to us. He didn't have to go down to that island—Severn put in for him, but he didn't have to go. He went of his own accord."

Sulgrave accepted this in silence, wondering if she suspected that he hadn't known until this very day that she and Dolfus had anything but the most casual acquaintance.

She returned to her earlier reminiscent tone. "Something went sour in him after Sevie died. First, it was just a subtle irritation with life, but later it seemed to gnaw at him. Our marriage couldn't satisfy him. His job couldn't satisfy him. Everything had been going so well up to then. He was on his way to flag rank, for a certainty. But after Sevie died, he couldn't get along with himself. He had trouble with his men—that's why he wanted Ben to be his Exec this time—Ben knew my husband and understood him. And of course Ben understood what Sevie meant to him, and what a terrible thing his death did to him. Ben was a sort of father confessor to Sevie when Ben was teaching at his school. That's all we heard for the first few months—all about this wonderful teacher named Dolfus. And when Sevie was drowned, it was almost as hard on Ben as it was on us. But it was never the same after that—I suppose it never can be—I wanted another child, but . . ." Sulgrave noticed that she was looking out of the window at nothing, and that her tone was rambling. He couldn't follow her in everything, but it didn't seem important that he follow, just that he understand and listen and let her talk herself out. ". . . and then came the business of running aground, and the inquiry . . . then it was . . . was . . . oh, he would drink too much . . . and little things, too. Sometimes, oh a lot of times, I'd be in bed with him, and wish it was like it was before . . . when he could . . . could . . . I tried to help him, but I couldn't. I failed him. You can't know what it's like to love a man, and want to . . . be a wife to him, be a wife in bed and make him feel like . . . like a . . . You don't know what a heartbreaking kind of love that is . . . you're too young to know how to love someone and hate them for not being able to love you as much . . . want you

84

as much in return. He just went sour inside. First the destroyer going aground, now he's dead . . . and mutiny. Do you understand what I mean when I say he went sour? Do you?"

"I think so," Sulgrave answered carefully. "But you'll have to tell me who Sevie is."

She glanced at him, surprised. "Sevie was Bonuso Severn Hake, Junior. His son." Then as though correcting herself, she said, "*My* son."

Sulgrave was so shocked that he couldn't move; it was as though the last astounding piece had fallen into the puzzle, making the picture recognizable and complete. So Dolfus the teacher had once taught Hake's son . . .

They rode in silence for a moment, until suddenly Vanna said, as though to herself, in a tone of empty bitterness, almost of scorn, "*He tried to make a man of him.*"

Her face twisted and she stiffened. Suddenly she turned on Sulgrave and buried her face in his shoulder, clinging to him till her knuckles were bloodless white. The silent convulsive jerking of her whole body was like a sudden fit, and it wasn't till he felt the first hot tears on his neck that he realized that she was simply crying. Then came the first ugly sob, a racking gasp of agony. He took her in his arms because she was in misery and words were useless, and held her. By the time they neared Washington she was long since asleep. When she awoke she wanted a drink; they stopped for a cocktail before going to her hotel.

When things were finally straightened out on the pier, Dolfus had the bugler muster the men again, and while Sulgrave stood by, lectured them. The men seemed not resentful, but chastened by their poor performance during the fire drill, and listened seriously as Dolfus ticked off his indictment. Then, knowing from their faces that the lesson had sunk in, he said no more. He stood silently before them a long moment, then very quietly dismissed them. They didn't run to their barracks as they usually did after inspection, like children released from school; instead they walked, talking quietly among themselves. For one thing, the Old Man was sore and they knew they hadn't heard the end of it.

After changing into dry clothes, Sulgrave started up the path to return the Commander's cutlass. Halfway up he met Orval, the colored boy who doubled as the Commander's steward, and returned his silent salute; something in the way Orval raised his eyebrows was enough to warn him of the Commander's mood. As he mounted the steps of the veranda, he felt a vague uneasiness in the hollow of his stomach; nor was the feeling allayed by the too-cheerful Come in that answered his knock on the open door frame.

Hake was standing naked in the middle of the floor, rubbing himself vigorously with a towel; wet footprints showed where he had just emerged from the shower in his private apartment.

"Sit down, Sulgrave," the Commander said, nodding to the chair behind his own desk. "I'll be with you in a minute." Ignoring Sulgrave's presence, he dried his genitals, then his feet, then flicked the towel over his shoulder and went out of the room. Sulgrave sat down uneasily, and laid the cutlass carefully on the desk. The Commander's nakedness embarrassed him; he could never be entirely casual in the naked presence of an older man, not even were the man his own father. Somehow, for him, it seemed vaguely taboo, a violation of his New Englander's sense of order and decorum. He gazed at the wet footprints on the board floor and turned his thoughts to something else.

For the first time he examined the cutlass. It was a businesslike weapon, stoutly and gracefully made, and obviously not of modern manufacture. From the nicks in the handle and guard, even though they had been nearly polished out, he deduced that the weapon had at one time probably seen action. So intent was he on his minute examination of the weapon that he didn't hear the Commander pad barefooted back into the room. He was wearing shorts.

"That sword was given to my wife's great-grandfather by Commodore John Rodgers, who was wearing it aboard the North Carolina when he received the first national salute ever given a United States flagship by the Regency of Tunis."

"How old is it, then?" Sulgrave asked.

"It was made by Nathan Starr in 1816, as a prototype for a contract of a thousand. He made some of the finest-edge weapons ever made." The Commander went back into his room and came out with the scabbard and a small picture frame which he'd taken off the wall. He blew the dust off it and handed it to Sulgrave; it contained an antique document, a letter, written in a bold hand. Sulgrave read it:

John Rodgers, Esqr.
Navy Board
Washington, D.C.

Agreeable to your directions & my promise, I have made two Ship Cutlasses & two Boarding Pikes and have sent you, by mail stage, one of each, inclosed in a small box. I was obliged to cut off the handle of the pike in order to stow it in the box.

Should you after examining these think it fit to let a contract, I should like it much and feel a pride in furnishing for our Navy, pikes and cutlasses equally to any that can be found in any Navy in the world.

I am Sir, Respectfully,
NATHAN STARR

Sulgrave handed the framed letter back to the Commander, who laid it atop the bookshelf. "You can see why I value it," he said. "I'd like to give it to the museum at the Academy, but I can't bring myself to part with it just yet. Perhaps I'll will it to them." Hake held out the scabbard to receive the blade.

Sulgrave picked up the weapon, looked at the mark NSTARR on the shoulder of the blade, then carefully sheathed it into its scabbard. Hake looked at the weapon with satisfaction, pride almost, then placed it also atop the bookcase. "Well, that's that," he said.

"I'm sorry I didn't return it before, but I didn't have my head about me," Sulgrave said.

Hake's face clouded, as though in remembrance of the water-logged scene of their last parting, then he said, "I didn't even notice it myself until I got up here."

Hake sat on the window ledge, his back to outside, and let

his bare feet dangle; it made Sulgrave feel uncomfortable to be sitting in the only chair.

The Commander's tone was suddenly faraway, almost wistful: "We all have our time of trial, this is mine. I feel like Prometheus, chained to this bloody rock, having my liver eaten out perpetually. But I suppose salvation will come."

Sulgrave said nothing, but remembered Dolfus' remark about Hake's Samson complex—it seemed closer to the point.

"I'm sure a man is made for better than this, don't you think?" the Commander continued.

"You're doing your best, sir, with what we've got."

Hake mused, "Yes, but they haven't given me very much, have they?"

"Perhaps if you requested . . ."

"No." His voice was suddenly decisive, as though he himself had been considering the same temptation. "I won't give them the satisfaction. That's just what they'd like—to have me come whining like a whipped dog." He rose and began pacing. "No, dammit. We've got to do it in spite of them." Suddenly he stopped and turned to Sulgrave. "What did you do to get stuck here?"

"I don't know what . . . that is, nothing, sir. At least, I don't *think* I did anything. I hadn't thought about it."

Hake grunted his curious noncommittal grunt and resumed pacing. "Well, you're better off not thinking about it. You can make yourself sick thinking." He muttered something unintelligible.

"I think your object lesson had its effect, sir. The men seemed quite sobered up by the failure of the drill. From what Lieutenant Dolfus said, they're not too proud of their performance. He gave them quite a chewing-out after you left."

Hake grunted again. "But no punishments, eh?"

"I haven't seen the report log, sir."

"Sulgrave, what do you think of as your destiny?"

The question took Sulgrave by surprise. "My destiny, sir?"

"Yes. What do you think you're destined to be in life?"

"I'd like to be a naval architect, that is unless we get into the war. Then I suppose I'll have to wait and see."

"It isn't time yet for war. The Great War will come after the half-century, when the white race will be threatened by the rest of the world."

"I don't understand, sir."

"Great historical events follow certain laws, just as great men always appear at certain crucial moments in time. Their appearance is always predicted."

"You mean like history repeating itself?"

"More subtle than that, Sulgrave. The laws of history are never understood by more than a handful of men in any given period. They are the true philosophers and the true prophets. There is nothing mystical about prophecy. It is a rational science. But it must be obscured from common eyes, because knowledge of the future is dangerous knowledge in the hands of brutes."

Sulgrave was startled. He looked at Hake as he paced back and forth, realizing that the man was revealing his inner preoccupation for the first time. This would explain his obsession with history.

"Gloria Dei est celare verbum," Hake said, continuing. "It took me ten years to understand that. Laws are deliberately obscured, for the sole purpose of making sure that only those astute enough to solve the riddle and wise enough to grasp its meaning can come into possession of its solution. This is why the great prophets always couch their words . . . why the great prophecies are open to double meanings. Don't you see? They must leave room for skeptics to doubt the word, otherwise the secret of the laws' very existence would be betrayed. As it is, a prophecy that comes true is always explained away either as a mere coincidence, or as a hindsight choice of only one of many possible interpretations of the original words. Do you follow me?"

Sulgrave nodded uncertainly.

"Sometimes the great seers are priests, sometimes prophets. Sometimes they are artists. It's different in every age. Sometimes they are great leaders, like Alexander or Napoleon. Military men. But always they know how to read the hidden word. Sometimes they make prophecies. Sometimes they simply read the prophecies that are already written in the literature."

"You mean that you *believe* in prophecy?"

Hake laughed, and Sulgrave was relieved. "I don't *believe* in prophecy, per se. What I do say is that the laws of history are probably understandable to those who are adept in the reading of hidden knowledge. It appears everywhere, but especially in the great texts—which of necessity are the works of even greater men. The more carefully you read, the more intensively you analyze, the more clear it becomes that there is a definite pattern in all the clues they plant. I'm at that stage now. I sense that there is an orderly pattern—even perhaps a whole system of knowledge—" Hake's enthusiasm suddenly subsided, as he shrugged his shoulders in a gesture of weariness. "The only trouble is that I only sense it. I don't *see* it. I haven't come far enough to be absolutely sure."

"Clues, sir? What kind of clues do you mean? Who are 'they'?"

Hake waved his hand vaguely. "Oh, all kinds. Some historical, some symbolic. Some of them are even playful, if you could call it that. Would you like to see what I finally tracked down this morning? I was up all night with it. That's why I was overtired this morning." He went straight to the bookcase without waiting for an answer. "It's harmless enough in itself, but it proves something I've suspected for a long time."

He took down a Bible and placed it on the desk before Sulgrave. "In fact," he said, "it rather pleases me to show this one to you, since I found it entirely on my own."

Sulgrave looked at the Bible in front of him, uncertain what was required of him.

"As you know," Hake began, pacing again with his head down, his bare feet slapping on the floor, "as you know, King James had the Bible translated by a group of poets and scholars of his day. Undoubtedly he was one of them, a man gifted with this special insight I've been talking about." Without stopping in his pacing, he continued. He seemed to be off in another world. "Now you may or you may not know that the pentagram is a key symbol in these matters. The number five is the sum of duality and completion, two being the number of duality and three being the number of completion, having beginning, middle and end. Five appears everywhere—in the five acts of tragedy, the five fingers of the hand—but no matter. Take my word for it that five is a crucial number." He glanced at Sulgrave and paused.

Sulgrave nodded compliantly, said nothing. *What in hell is this?*

"Open to the Book of Psalms. Look at Psalm Five."

Sulgrave picked up the Bible and leafed through until he found the Psalms, put his finger on the fifth one.

"Now read the first five words."

Sulgrave read aloud, " 'Give ear to my words.' "

"Now, what is the next psalm whose digits total five? Ignore the fourteenth, for the moment."

Sulgrave thought a moment. "You mean two plus three? The Twenty-third Psalm?"

"Right. Turn to it. Now count down to the fifty-fifth word and tell me what it is."

Sulgrave counted to himself—is he crazy?—finally said, "*Will.* The fifty-fifth word is *will.*"

"Now, double the number of the Psalm."

"Twenty-three plus twenty-three is forty-six."

Hake didn't look up from his pacing. "Turn to it, the Forty-sixth Psalm. Count to the forty-sixth word. What is it?"

Sulgrave counted, feeling a little stupid for not seeing what it was all about. "The forty-sixth word in the Forty-sixth Psalm is *shake.* Shake. I don't see what you're getting at."

"Never mind, you will. Now count forty-six words backwards from the end. Skip the word 'selah,' of course. That's just a musical direction. What do you get?"

After a moment Sulgrave looked up. "The forty-sixth word from the end is 'spear.'"

Hake looked at him expectantly, but Sulgrave continued to look uncomprehending.

"Don't you see it, Sulgrave?" Hake asked, smiling triumphantly. "Shake. Spear. The man who wrote Hamlet translated the Psalms!"

Sulgrave's mouth opened—he was uncertain as to how to react—but before he could say anything Hake was off again.

"Shakespeare was a tragedian—five acts. His name is twice five—five letters in shake, five in spear—which total can be represented as either fifty-five or ten. Now what is the total of the two digits in the Forty-sixth Psalm."

"Four plus six? Ten."

"Now turn to Isaiah. How many times five is Shakespeare's name again?"

"Twice."

"Look at the second chapter of Isaiah. Square ten and subtract ten. What do you get?"

"One hundred minus ten: Ninety."

"Count to the ninetieth word from the end. What is it?"

Sulgrave lost count once and had to start again. Finally he looked up and said, "I see. It's 'shake' again."

"Now what was the number of the psalm where his name previously appeared?"

"Forty-six."

"Add forty-six—which digits total ten, remember—add forty-six to the ninety you got by subtracting ten from its second power. What do you get?"

"Ninety plus forty-six is—let's see—a hundred and thirty-six?"

"You're catching on. From the beginning."

Sulgrave counted not out of doubt but merely to satisfy the pleasure of Hake's eyes. It took a long time and Hake turned to look out the window. Finally Sulgrave looked up, tried to hit the right tone. "Yes, it's right. How in the world did you ever figure this thing out?"

"Never mind that. Read the whole passage."

Sulgrave turned to the Bible and read, " 'And he shall judge among the nations, and shall rebuke many people: and they shall beat their swords into plowshares, and their spears into pruninghooks; nation shall not lift up sword against nation, neither shall they learn war any more.' "

Hake said, "Obviously Shakespeare was an adept. One of our great ones."

"You don't think it's merely coincidence, do you?"

Hake laughed. "What do you think?"

"I admit it's very extraordinary," Sulgrave said, scratching the back of his neck.

Hake gave him a knowing smile. "That's just an example

94

of the playful sort of clue I was telling you about. I was all night on that one, and it wasn't till this morning that I saw how it fitted together."

"What made you look for it in the first place?"

Hake smiled. "Other clues," he said, deliberately mysterious. "It does no good being told. You'll never become an adept until you learn to find them for yourself."

In the silence, Sulgrave noticed that Hake seemed to be brooding on something again. Finally the Commander said, "I want you to ask me a question?"

"A question?"

"I want you to ask me what made me ask for a fire drill today of all days."

"I thought perhaps you'd noticed last Saturday that the hoses had been disconnected, and that you planned it as an object lesson."

Hake shook his head as though sadly bewildered. "No," he said, "I didn't notice. In fact, I didn't think of having a fire drill until I was walking down the path with you this morning. I don't know what put the idea into my head. If any good came of it, it was merely by accident."

Sulgrave wasn't sure what to say, said nothing.

"You know what I'm thinking, don't you?" Hake said.

"No, sir."

"What made you think of using my sword to cut that hose? You could have just as easily grabbed a fire ax off one of the stanchions."

"I don't know, sir. I guess it was the nearest thing. It was your sword that gave me the idea in the first place."

"And you didn't feel you should have asked my permission?"

"Well, sir, I guess I just acted on reflex."

Hake shook his head. " 'They shall beat their swords into

95

plowshares . . .' " Then he sighed heavily. "I'll never know what possessed me to have that fire drill. There's a meaning in it somewhere, but where?"

Suddenly Hake stood up. "Mister Sulgrave, have a good weekend. I'll see you Monday morning."

With that he went into his living quarters and closed the door behind him. Sulgrave stood uncertainly a moment, experiencing an uneasy sense of relief, glanced at the open Bible in his hands. He closed it and put it back in its place in the bookcase. The book next to it, he noticed, was a well-used morocco-bound copy of Hamlet. He almost felt like tiptoeing out.

Suddenly the Commander came out again. "I forgot one part of it," he said. "Did you notice that in Isaiah Two, the 'spears' were plural? That would require more than one 'shake,' wouldn't it? Well, count twenty-three—the number of the psalm where his first name, Will, appears—count twenty-three from the end and you'll find the other 'shake.' Thus the name appears twice in the same place, that is, in the second chapter of Isaiah—which is why you have to raise his name to the second power of its natural number. Go ahead, count back twenty-three. The word 'wherein' can be counted as two words. Then you might read the two verses that contain the 'shakes' that match the 'spears.' Then think of what we're doing on this island."

Hake watched Sulgrave until he took the Bible out again, then said, "Tell me Monday what you think of it. I'm going to take a nap." He went back into his room and closed the door, and Sulgrave could hear him going around closing the louvers of his room against the sun; he leafed back and forth looking for Isaiah, suddenly felt foolish, irritated with Hake. But curiosity prevailed.

Counting back twenty-three words, he found the other "shake"; then he read the two verses twice over to himself.

> 19 And they shall go into the holes
> of the rocks, and into the caves of the
> earth, for fear of the Lord, and for
> the glory of his majesty, when he
> ariseth to shake terribly the earth.

The other seemed almost identical.

> 21 To go into the clefts of the rocks,
> and into the tops of the ragged rocks,
> for fear of the Lord, and for the glory
> of his majesty, when he ariseth to
> shake terribly the earth.

"You mean how can I be sure, now that he's gone?"

She fell silent a moment, her face pensive, deeply serious, as though she was searching for precise words. Immediately he realized that he'd asked her a question she had already crucially asked herself. She didn't look at him, but kept her gaze fixed on her cigarette as though mesmerized by the endless ribbon of smoke unspooling from the base of the soft gray ash. She'd finished her martini.

"Once you've loved someone, you don't fall out of love. You simply learn to hate. You still have your love inside you and it can never die before you die, because it's a part of you just as your lungs and your bowels are a part of you. Hate can submerge love, can drown it the way a tide drowns a rock, but the love is still there just as real and just as solid as it always was. The hate simply counterbalances it. And when the reason for hating is gone—when that someone is gone and can no longer hurt you—then hate gets off the seesaw without warning and down you come with a crash in love again. And you hurt. That's how you know."

He's a nut
Commander or no Commander . . .
Jig jog. Down the Admiral's path.
Completely off his head. But he is.
Is a man crazy because he believes some-
thing, or only when he tries to prove it?
Skully says he's strange, didn't say crazy.
Maybe
If I try to prove it.
try to prove it
That crazy sword. Ride a cocked hat to
Barbary Cross.
If you have to prove, you don't believe.
He can't believe
. . . whole island crazy, we're all in-
sane.
He wants to believe it.
Whoa, now. I'm trying to laugh it off.
Trying too hard, too quick. Vulnerable,
that's right, to fear.
Something's very wrong. Maybe he's
right.
Is a man crazy who can't believe in
something?
Hungry. Am I capable of crazy?
Forget it.
Ask Skully, little crazy too.
He's a nut.
Commander or no Commander . . .
Home again home again.

■

"Stop hogging the bottle."

"The Commander's sure interested in numbers, isn't he."

"Ah, Columbus discovers America."

"I see. It doesn't worry you?"

"You worried about being dead, son?"

"Aren't you?"

"We're too scared to worry, laddie. It's fear keeps us young."

"*Who's* hogging the bottle?"

"I who am about to, salute you."

"Pour me a salute."

There was more to Little Misery than Sulgrave had suspected. Separated from the minuscule village by a nearly impassable sand road—Dolfus: "Take your shoes off, man, before you bog down completely . . ."—was a part of the island that had obviously once been a small coco plantation, now revitalized to serve the additional function of a sort of picnic ground. Sulgrave learned that his host for the afternoon was the enterprising Surinamese barber, who was also the island's doctor, notary and unofficial mayor. They received his greeting as they paid their admission. It was Sulgrave's introduction into island society.

"I think it's about time," Skully said. "I've got one of mine fighting this afternoon."

The sandy track was heavily footprinted where they entered the grassy coco grove through a gap in the impenetrable sea grape which grew wild and surrounded the place. In the center of the grove was a cockpit with crudely made seats, sagging planks that were raised in three tiers around all four sides. It was the size of a bandstand, with a shaky roof that heightened the resemblance. All around the pit, tethered to stakes at the shaded foot of each coco tree, were brightly plumed roosters, fighting cocks. Several dozen T-shirted men from the base were lounging near an improvised bar, a plank laid across two packing crates, from behind which a spindly mocha-colored woman Sulgrave had never seen before was dispensing beer. All around were women of various ages and degrees of color; all were strangers to Sulgrave's eye.

"Where do they all come from?" he asked Dolfus.

Dolfus pointed through the trees for answer. Sulgrave looked and saw the rough masts of a native schooner standing above the wall of sea grape. Dolfus said, "If customers can't come to the merchant, the merchant comes to the customer. True love always finds a way."

"Where do they come from?"

Dolfus shrugged. "There are several dozen islands within two days' sail from here, many more beyond that. These people use sloops and schooners as you and I use taxis and subways. They think nothing of sleeping and cooking on an open deck."

Looking around the rim of the grove, Sulgrave saw several other masts, shorter ones whose main trucks barely showed above the heavy sea grape—these would be sloops. "I'll be damned," he said.

"Saturday afternoon is for officers, warrants, chiefs, and petty officers first and second. Tomorrow for all other ranks."

Sulgrave laughed. "Rank has its privileges."

A coffee-colored man whom Sulgrave had seen several times with the Surinam barber came up cradling a large fighting cock. "You gonta fight 'im today, mon."

"Yes, mon. Whachu t'ink," Dolfus said, falling easily into the accent.

"Got 'im match with Randy's bird. He only bird his weight left. Randy say he fight with without spurs. What you say?"

"Didn't bring any heavy birds this trip?"

"No, mon. They all mos' frightful-lookin' chickens this week. Ain't none a match for yo' two. My hurt she leg las' week."

"Then let's go without spurs, or I won't have anyone to work up my bird on. Same rules as last week, O.K.?"

The man nodded and went off to get ready.

Dolfus explained to Sulgrave that there was a chronic shortage of birds, and that sometimes they fought them without spurs against a time limit. "It's not real cockfighting. But . . ."

"Who makes the decision?"

"Mr. Sung. He's the expert around here. Let's get a beer."

The beer was cooled in a makeshift well and was not cheap. Sulgrave asked, "Where does it come from?"

Dolfus shrugged. "Same place the other commodities do, I guess."

Sulgrave sipped silently at his beer, which was bitter and lukewarm, and stared around at the unsuspected life of the place, wondering if the Commander knew of its existence. The tethered cocks crowed raucous challenges to each other; he'd often heard them faintly at dawn when the wind was right, never noticing that there seemed to be a disproportionate number of roosters for such a small place as Little Misery. If anything, he'd dismissed them as a few roosters that did a great deal of crowing. But tethered under the trees were at least three dozen that he could count.

"That was my handler you saw," Dolfus said. "He imports them and fattens them up, then sells them to the boys. Mr. Sung owns the pit and holds the money."

There were twelve fights that afternoon, all with spurs but the last. The men and their fancy women crowded the pit and stomped their feet on the sagging planks and shouted out their bets. Half the time, Sulgrave watched the crowd rather than the birds, undecided as to which was the better spectacle. The birds all had names: Red Demon, Toolshed, Signifier, Potluck, Rocking Horse, Compressor (who fought Jackhammer and lost), Skylark, Admiral Luck, Toenail— Sulgrave tried to remember them all, and indeed when discussing the fights afterward, remembered a great many of them. He'd picked up the names by simply listening to the money-waving cries of the crowd; bets were made at any point in the match by holding up a sum and shouting the offered odds and the name of the bird, until a taker shouted agreement. Mr. Sung stood at the side of the pit, taking the money as it was passed to him and keeping track in his head of the bettors and amounts. He operated with all the aplomb of a croupier, and never once in paying off to the winners did he come out short or over. He was simply the clearing house through which money flowed as it changed hands. During the fights, trays of beer flowed in as empty bottles flowed out from the wildly waving shouting sweating crowd. The incredible thing to Sulgrave was that the stomping, swaying structure didn't cave in completely; several times, at the heights, the excitement became totally hysterical. Whenever a favorite bird was downed or was on the receiving end of a "marriage"—pronounced Frenchwise and referring to a bird's being impaled by one of the needlesharp steel spurs, a situation requiring separation by the handlers—at several such times the attendant frenzy was such that Sulgrave was certain the frail structure would collapse on the instant.

But it didn't, and he stayed with Dolfus to the end. The crowd booed good-naturedly when they saw that Skully's and Randy's birds would fight without spurs, but they bet anyway. Mr. Sung's judgment was disputed, but accepted; within the time allotted, he called the match a draw.

When the afternoon was over, the air was edged with the smell of baking fish—Sulgrave learned from Dolfus that a fish fry would bridge the gap between afternoon and evening, but that they wouldn't stay for it. Dolfus had to get ready for his "art class."

"Would you like to get a little rockdust in your ears?" he asked Sulgrave. "We'll go back and chow down first."

"I'm not sure I can handle a jackhammer, but I'd like to come along and try." And he was elated beyond all reason.

When they left the coco grove, the sun was lowering toward the sea, and the place was calm, peaceful, waiting. The smell of cooking, everyone hungry. A few men were coming back from swimming, skylarking among themselves snapping at each other with towels. At the far end of the grove several women, supervised by Mr. Sung, were working over the dozen open braziers that studded the ground like smoking mushrooms. The smell of food was in itself a pleasure to be enjoyed, and men lazed aimlessly about the grove, talking and laughing in groups around the women. To one side, three men sat with their backs around a palm tree. One played a slow thin melody on his harmonica, as around them, barefooted on the accidental grass, a girl danced bemused, as though talking to herself.

Sulgrave saw Dolfus stiffen, like a sleeper aroused from a dream; the girl saw them in the same instant, and ran.

As they left the grove, Sulgrave noticed Arielle again, darting around the edge of sea grape hiding from them. Instantly he felt uneasy. Dolfus muttered an oath and started walking quickly, leaving the pleasant afternoon in the grove behind him. He walked ahead of Sulgrave, saying nothing. He was silent all the way to Mother-in-Trouble's shack. Sulgrave was sweating from the pace.

"Wait here."

Sulgrave waited. Dolfus silently approached the shack, slipped inside without a sound.

Suddenly from inside the shack there was a surprised shout

of pain and Mother-in-Trouble tumbled out holding her back. Dolfus was behind her swinging his belt like a strap.

"You get that girl away from there or I'll beat you white. You know what I've told you."

"You don't proper her," the woman said. She looked very angry, yet guilty before Dolfus' wrath.

"Did you send her down there? If you did, woman . . ."

"I aren't see her all day."

"Do you know what Randy will do to you if he finds out you let her down there. He'll . . ."

"That black mon no her father."

"He's the closest thing she ever had to one, you mean-fisted old money grub. You want me to tell him what you just said?"

She backed down, still rubbing her back. "Non, 'sieur."

"You going down there and get her and keep her here?"

"Oui, 'sieur."

"Allez, donc. Vite. Je vais envoyer Randy plus tard pour vous surveiller. Comprende, Señora?"

"Si, Señor."

With that she waddled off in the direction they had just come from, not looking at Sulgrave as she passed him. Dolfus started walking toward the cut, putting his belt back through its loops as he went. Sulgrave followed him twenty paces behind, not catching up until they reached the boat.

"What was that all about?" Sulgrave asked.

Dolfus only shook his head sullenly and wrapped the starting rope around the flywheel. "Ignore it," he said, and yanked viciously. The unmuffled noise of the outboard ended conversation, and they crossed the cut each looking straight ahead.

"You mean the old woman tried to beat her?"

"After Randy and him left, yessir."

"What did this? Mon, look at that welt."

"What she hit you with, girl?"

"She got pizzle from man on boat this morning."

"What's she mean?"

"A bull's pizzle. They dry them for flogs."

"You no tell her I tol' you." The girl bit her lip. "She drink now. You no tell Skully?"

"Skully won't let her hurt you," Sulgrave said.

The girl's eyes flicked toward Sulgrave, then down at the floor. She giggled privately. Sulgrave watched her, but she wouldn't look up at him. He felt fooled, suddenly clumsy.

"Will you take me to dinner?" She spoke over her shoulder as she filled out the registration card. The desk clerk brought his palm down on the bell; a rich ding sounded; a bellboy stepped forward from between potted philodendrons.

"Of course. I'd be delighted."

She finished her signature without flourish, and turned around to face him. "Will you come up and wait while I change? I'm very hungry."

"Anything you say, ma'am."

"You're being very amenable all of a sudden. Have you become resigned to your fate?"

Sulgrave glanced at her as they walked toward the elevators, saw her smile, said nothing.

In the elevator they said nothing. While they followed the bellhop through the plushly carpeted corridor, they said nothing. When they entered the room, he took the two bags and tipped the boy, who left closing the door behind him. Sulgrave carried her luggage into the bedroom and put it down, wondering why she hadn't told him earlier that the bags were in the trunk of the limousine. The trip was less impromptu than she'd made it seem. He stood up, found himself facing her. She was removing her gloves, watching him.

"You've been a very good boy," she said, "so far. And very sweet. Now sit down and talk to me while I change."

He sat down on the bed and watched her as she opened the suitcases and began putting her things in order. The dresses she hung in the closet, the rest she apportioned carefully among the drawers of the dresser. The items from her vanity case she carried into the bathroom and arrayed one by one on the plate-glass shelf above the sink. He watched her through the open door.

But they didn't talk. She seemed absorbed in what she was doing, and he was completely absorbed in watching her. Finally she went to the closet and took out a dress, a dark blue one of watered silk, and held it up for his approval.

"All right?" she asked.

"Very nice."

"I got it on sale," she said irrelevantly.

She laid it carefully across the foot of the bed. Then, as though he weren't in the room at all, she crossed to the mirror and stood before it, as though appraising herself. For a long moment she studied her reflection. Then she reached up behind her back and unzipped her dress to the waist, pulled it off her arms, and stepped out of it. Her shoulders seemed even more whitely naked for the black slip she was wearing. She held up the dress she'd just taken off and cocked her head to one side as she examined it. Then she turned it inside out and threw it at the bed; it fell short and slid off onto the rug. She made no move to pick it up, but simply stood looking at it impassively, her arms folded.

"I hate black," she said.

"But *why* . . ."

"Sometimes I feel . . . listen to me now."

"I'm listening."

". . . obsessed. I dream about my big rock head at night sometimes. It's the only sensible thing I'm doing on this island. It won't hurt anyone. It's not for war or for peace, but for pastime. When this rock blows sky-high we'll all go with it, but my old statue will have the last laugh, or last cry, depending whether we're men or boys. Listen to me, don't interrupt! You think I started that sculpture just to provide recreation for the boys? Like hell. I started carving to provide Creation with something new, something that never existed before. It's the least a man can do before he goes. You ask me if the skipper is liable to crack up—I ask you: Are *you* sane? If so, why did you join a military organization? I know why I joined and it's none of your business, but why did you join? At the moment, Hake is who we've got, and until all men are angels it will never be any different. We were and are supposed to have three more white officers here—think of what that could mean. Are you deaf, dumb and blind to what's going on here? You don't think these boys know that they get the garbage and sweat details in this man's navy? How often do you see white troops loading ammunition? No, that's a black job. It'll change, of course, but not before tomorrow, not before the next day, either. You don't think men don't know that? How would you feel? You think they're happy just because they laugh, just because they sing and dance and get drunk—innocent savages. But I tell you you're sitting on more than one powder keg. There's men on this island who would rather kill you than sit at your table. They know what's going on here. They know that certain death hangs over their head—it hangs from a single white thread. Hake knows the risks, but he's trying to do a job on urgent orders. They want this place built, and built fast. He's doing exactly what has to be done: taking a risk. He won't put in for increased personnel because he knows he won't get it. And why ask for more men and risk more lives than he's already risking? He reads his books, and probably he's a fool as well as a gambler. I've almost come to hate him, and at times even tried to undermine him. I can tell myself he's not sanctified, and he's not. But a war isn't sanctified either, except as legal murder, so how can I fret about whether he'll stay in his right mind when the whole goddamned world is going crazy? Someone's got to stop the Tamerlanes. Washington wants this built in a hurry because we are going to war—the irony is that Hake can't even believe *that*, because he thinks war means the end of the world. Is that so crazy? Am I so sane for not deserting on a native sloop? The best I can do is to try to balance destruction with creation. I work with my hands to stay sane, to stay alive. I impose order on this chaos by carving it out of a hundred-ton rock with an airhammer. If it helps to stay alive, I'll try to do it . . . shit, it's the least I can do. Shit on suicide. We'll all be dead soon enough."

"I had no business asking the question."

"Forget it. I had no business answering it."

As long as he lived Sulgrave would never forget his first sight of the Garden of Nothing Doing. The name was a corruption of "North Dune" or "Norther Dane," which were variant names for the long, off-lying shoal and its terminating sand island. According to Dolfus, who had it from Mr. Sung, the bar got its name from a Danish privateer who, after a daring raid, used it to escape a pursuing French man-o'-war by luring the deeper-draft vessel aground on it. The first white inhabitants of Manacle Rock were the marooned survivors of the French wreck, which explained some of the French names for local landmarks. But whatever the real origin of the northernmost point of Manacle Rock, in the quick appreciation of the new arrivals, "Nawtha Doan"— which is how the local fishermen pronounced it—became, inevitably, "Nuthin' Doin'."

The Garden of Nothing Doing was a group of tombstone-like rocks on a flat acre that was cut like a giant foothold into the steep side of Manacle Rock halfway up from the boiling sea. Time, weather and earthquakes had shaken loose the great shards of rock from above, and had plunged their slivered ends into the hard ledge soil where they had remained, upright and mysterious, stony sentries looking out to sea. Some were just slivers, thinner than a man and not much taller; others progressively larger and squatter. But the largest, a huge brute of a rock that stood behind the others, towered to the height of a two-story house. This monster had apparently once been the brow of the overhang from which its smaller brethren had earlier fallen. Centuries of vegetation had built up the earth around them so that now they looked as though they grew from it, like weird cacti or burnt tree trunks, and though some of them leaned drunkenly askew the largest among them were perfectly vertical. Any that had toppled over were long since buried beneath the ageless manufacture of goatweed and guinea grass that carpeted the eerie garden.

Wild goats, possibly descended from the live larder of the outwitted French man-o'-war, still roamed the island; it was these who had discovered the easiest route to the place. All the bulldozer had done was to widen and level their track; thus a very passable road followed a gradual rise around the sides of the island until it came to an impassable halt a few yards before and slightly above the "garden." Here the road was widened into a turnaround, and it was here that Dolfus and Sulgrave found the unattended compressor already chugging away as they arrived.

Dolfus led the way, following the air hose, to the top of a rocky rise where the hose disappeared over the edge. It had still been light when they left the base, but the rapid deepening of sundown sea so drained the sky of its remaining light that it was dusk as Dolfus started down the fixed iron ladder that curved down out of sight over the rock.

The ladder was ingeniously made out of scrap ends of concrete-reinforcing rods, welded together and fastened into holes drilled in the rock. Sulgrave was so intent on examining the ladder as it went up through his hands that he wasn't aware of the activity around him until he felt sod beneath his feet and turned around. The jackhammer suddenly ceased. It was the first time he'd ever seen the place, but the first impression was enough to make itself indelible.

Since the place was shadowed from the west, it seemed already night down here and a scattered dozen Coleman lan-

113

terns hissed out a brilliant greenish-white light that cast a dozen crisscrossed sets of angled shadows through the jutting grove of rocks. Because of the rockdust that hung illumined in the still air, the shadows seemed like a labyrinth of black solids, ghostly intersecting walls through which men seemed to emerge as they came to greet Dolfus.

As they walked past the lanterns, their own shadows turned like black beacons in the luminous dust, bounding over the dreamlike ground and up the walls in a wild ballet to the hissing silence. The unreal shapes were matched by the denizens of the place—Sulgrave saw that they were wearing snout-like dust masks and goggles and had ordinary navy hats inside out over their ears. Most of the men were stripped to the waist; they were no longer black but gray with powdered rock. It seemed for one dizzy instant that his sense impressions were dangerously awry; everything seemed amplified to abnormal intensity: the shadows, the glowing air, the extraordinarily loud hissing of the gasoline lanterns . . .

Then he realized. It wasn't just the lanterns—it was leakage from the air hose! There was nothing oversensitive about his hearing, the hissing *was* loud. The split second of unreality passed, and everything returned to normal. He even distinguished the soft chugging of the compressor from the road. Shadows became shadows; rocks, rocks; and as the first man raised his mask and goggles, his grin seemed as human as ever.

Suddenly, from above his head to the left, the jackhammer resumed its deafening metallic stutter, and Sulgrave looked up to see two men suspended from a bosun's chair working on the face of the largest rock, a lantern hanging seemingly in midair over their head. For a moment it wasn't clear what they were working on, but stepping back for a total view Sulgrave saw that the entire rock had been sculpted into a huge head on narrow shoulders. Everything was finished but the mouth, and that was what they were working on now. The mouth had been roughed in with white paint and was half open and turned down at the corners like a classical mask of tragedy. As the jackhammer cut away the white-painted area of stone, a spew of dust and chips dribbled steadily off the half-formed lower lip like gray spittle onto the ground below.

Sulgrave felt someone nudging his shoulder and turned to find Dolfus offering him goggles and respirator. Dolfus put his own mask on and showed Sulgrave by gestures how to adjust the dust bag over his nose and mouth. The jackhammer stopped as the men shifted position, one man holding the hammer, the other playing the block and tackle from which the ponderous tool was suspended. The yammering resumed, working now in short bursts as the yawning maw tapered toward the lower left corner of the mouth. When finished, this oral cavern would be nearly large enough for a man to stand in.

Dolfus was involved in a discussion of detail with the men working on the great head, when Sulgrave decided to make use of the lull to see what the other men were doing around the place. Each man seemed to be working, sometimes with one or more helpers, all with hand tools, on his own private statue. The variety of fantastic shapes was bewildering: a fish standing on its tail; a rooster head crowing skyward; a fire hydrant that might have come off a New York street; an indefinable shape that looked like a squat totem pole (he learned later that this was the rock which beginners were allowed to practice on); an eight-foot-tall replica of someone's forefinger; and by all odds the favorite idea, the female nude—here the results were not so successful, suffering as they did from a certain bald literalism in details of their anatomy.

"Would you like to try your hand?" It was Dolfus, come up behind him, his respirator hung around his neck, his goggles up on his forehead; a night breeze was rising from the sea and partially clearing the air of dust. Sulgrave did the same with his mask and goggles.

"How long did it take to do all this?" Sulgrave asked.

"The boys have been at it awhile. They used to come up just to help. Now it's their baby. Did you see my fish?"

"The one standing on its tail? Yes. I thought it was very good."

"This rock is fairly soft compared to what we have down below. Makes a good recreation. Some of the boys come up here by themselves when they're off during the day. A couple of them are really good at it. We'll probably finish roughing out Laughing Boy by tonight."

"Is that what you call him? Laughing Boy?"

"We flipped a coin to decide whether to turn the mouth up or down. He looks pretty good, don't you think?"

Sulgrave looked back at the enormous head looming up out of the falling dust and light; the men dangling at its lip looked as though they were being devoured. The airhammer was quiet at that moment and one of the men was leaning into the cavernous mouth, holding the lantern as the other changed the tool bit. Overhead the sky was a rich night blue and the first stars were out. In the distance the compressor chugged rhythmically.

"What do you mean you'll be finished 'roughing out'? It looks nearly finished to me."

"There's always something more we can do. The object is not to finish him, but to give the boys something to do. Next week we'll go to work with hand tools, detailing the eyes and such. After that we can put in wrinkles. And if we're still here after *that* we can tattoo him, I suppose. The main thing is to have something ahead of us all the time. Finishing is secondary."

"How come the Old Man lets you use the tools?"

Dolfus shrugged. "What does it cost the taxpayer? Nothing. We use old bits, an old hammer, and as for that one-lunger compressor—the boys salvaged it from the junk heap. Some of these boys don't want to spend all their time in the bushes with those inter-island grunts. You want them to sit on their hands till they crack up?"

"What ever gave you the idea anyway? I mean to make statues."

"Did you ever see Easter Island? I saw it once when we were on a hydrographic cruise. When I saw these rocks I thought of those statues on Easter Island." Dolfus smiled and looked toward the big statue as the jackhammer started again. "Laughing Boy will give them something to think about."

"Give who something to think about?"

Dolfus gestured toward the sea. "Anybody. Who cares who? But by God they'll wonder when they see him. You haven't seen him in the daytime yet."

At that moment the hammer stopped and Sulgrave heard three short beeps of an automobile horn from up on the turnaround. Dolfus looked at his watch. "Orval's here with the beer. He's early."

The two men were already halfway up the ladder, and the men on the statue pulled up the jackhammer and began lowering themselves to the ground. A few men continued to chip away, but most of them dropped their tools and gathered expectantly around the foot of the ladder. The compressor wheezed to a stop, and the hissing of the hose ceased

117

as someone opened the blow-off valve on the reservoir. The two men came down the ladder, each with a case of beer on his shoulder. Orval BlueEyes followed them down.

Orval came directly out to where Dolfus and Sulgrave were standing. He looked uncertainly at Sulgrave before speaking.

Dolfus said, "It's all right, Orval. What's the matter? The Old Man?"

Orval nodded. "He was playin' his gramophone when I left." Orval was a young man with a cook's rating, too young and too concerned to make a secret of his anxiety. Dolfus took the news soberly, thought a moment.

"How long ago?" Dolfus asked.

"Jes' a little while ago. That's why I come straight up here."

"Did you get Randy?"

"Yessuh. He keepin' his ear out."

Dolfus seemed to relax slightly. "Well, there shouldn't be anything to worry . . ." Abruptly he halted in mid-sentence, looked narrowly at Orval as though he'd just grasped what Orval was leaving unsaid. "You don't mean that she's up there again . . ."

It all came out in a flood. "I told that girl if I caught her hangin' 'round I'd come down on her with both feet the nex' time. But I had to go down to the commissary after dinner, and I thought sure he was goin' to sleep. He ain't been to sleep since yesterday morning."

"How do you know she's with him?"

"I don't know for sure, but Randy says one of the boys saw her down by your house a while ago, after you and Lieutenant Sulgrave left." He dropped his eyes and mumbled, "He playing his gramophone in his bedroom."

Dolfus took off his hat and distractedly passed his hand

over his bald head, put the hat back on and squared it viciously. "Orval, I don't know whether to throttle you, the old woman, or . . ."

"I was only gone for a while, suh. But that child is a very devil, you know that. And I was sure he was goin' to sleep, what with all the liquor that man drunk."

"Well, there's going to be hell to pay."

"Oh, I know how he gets. You don't have to tell me none. I still have a lump on my head from the last . . ." Orval stopped and glanced anxiously at Sulgrave.

Dolfus finished for him. ". . . from the last time we put him to bed. I know." He turned resignedly and faced Sulgrave. "You'd find out for yourself sooner or later. This doesn't happen often, but when it does it's a ball breaker."

"You coming back with me, suhs?"

"What for?" Dolfus asked dully. "The trouble won't come till later. No, you go back and do what Randy tells you. He can manage him better than I can. If you can get that little fool out of there, get her out. I'll be up in plenty of time. How much has he drunk already?"

"He finished a new bottle from this afternoon on. I couldn't get him to eat much, either."

"All right. You go on back. And remember if a word of this gets out I'll turn your ass inside out, you hear me, sailor?"

"I won't say nothing, suh."

Dolfus clapped his shoulder, smiled. "And don't let him rile you none. Just pretend you're white, like I do."

After Orval left, Dolfus fell into a mood of listless resignation. He and Sulgrave sat drinking beer in a pair of weathered canvas deck chairs at a point overlooking the sea, far out of earshot of the men. A late moon was rising, and they sat silently watching it for a long while. Then Dolfus began to talk, tiredly, without rancor, like a man reconstructing an accident.

"In the beginning, I'm sure the old woman put her up to it—the only thing she cares about is money and her troubles. She seems to be avenging herself on her children for all the sins of her own miserable life. Children mature faster down in these islands—at twelve there's nothing they don't know—and they have a totally different attitude toward things. Sex is a game children play from the time they're old enough to amuse themselves."

"Well, if it's not a violation of local custom, what does it matter? I'll admit that fourteen is . . ."

"It matters that he wasn't raised in the same way—it's not a game for him. It's a matter of life and death. As for her being fourteen—that's what she says she is. She's probably younger."

"She's a very striking creature all the same."

"That coloring comes from her father. From what I can make out, she's a quadroon. If she had half a chance to grow up decently, she'd be a beautiful woman. And she's intelligent. But although she's learned to mimic adult forms, mentally she's still a child. Here, look at this . . ."

Dolfus took out his wallet and extracted a folded piece of paper which he spread on his knees. He struck his cigarette lighter and it flared briefly in the light breeze, just long enough for Sulgrave to see a picture of a large doll: GOLDILOCKS DOLL; CRIES REAL TEARS, SAYS "MAMA." Dolfus closed the lighter and refolded the paper.

"She tore it out of an old Sears and Roebuck catalogue. Asked me to get it for her."

"Are you going to get it?"

"I ordered it a month ago. It'll be here on the next ship probably."

Sulgrave shook his head. "It's a contrast, I'll admit. Playing with dolls, making love . . ."

"If it only was that simple. If it was just a simple matter of making love, but he . . ." Dolfus turned his hands up empty, looking for a way out of the dark knowledge that suddenly enveloped both of them. "He just tortures himself with her."

"You mean he can't make it?"

"Yes, yes. Forget I told you about it. I feel bad enough just knowing, without telling you. But you're not the only one who knows. I had to threaten the old woman with a beating to keep her from telling everyone in creation. She thought it was a huge joke. I'd like to go up there and wring that damned child's neck. I wish I didn't have to keep calling her a child."

"It's a delicate situation."

"He abets it, of course. But only when he's too drunk to remember anything about it the next day. I'm not sure he remembers anything at all. I've never seen anything like it. He'll go for a month without a drink or a whimper. Then he works himself into a state of nervous exhaustion by staying up and reading all night, never going out of the house, never eating properly. Sometimes he just drinks and quietly passes out, and that's all right. But other times . . ." he looked at the luminous dial of his watch "—well, we'll soon know."

"Look, you think he's *already* cracked, don't you."

"Psycho?" Dolfus didn't look up. There was a slight pause. "What makes you so worried all of a sudden?"

"I don't know. Today he was talking about prophecy, and hidden knowledge . . . he almost had me . . . In fact he showed me something in the Bible that . . ."

"I don't know," Dolfus said flatly. "So he's started that

affair with you, has he? The Armageddon of the white race, and all that?"

"Well—" Sulgrave found himself cut off sharply.

"*If* the white race doesn't survive, it will be because on their own terms they don't deserve to survive. They've set their own terms for salvation—let them live up to them or be damned." Dolfus was suddenly truculent. He jumped to his feet and threw his empty beer bottle out into the night. It disappeared over the edge without a sound and into the sea. "I'm *sick* of these episcopate pricks who don't know the meaning of charity—they're trapped in their own contraceptive longings after nobility. They can't even love their human selves, so how can they intelligently love humanity? Let him learn to sing and keep his pecker up, *then* we can ponder the mysteries."

At the sound of Dolfus' raised voice, the men stopped talking and turned to look. Dolfus again made the angry gesture of squaring his hat. Then, like a man who's said his piece at a meeting, he sat down.

"No, I don't think he's commitably insane," Dolfus said finally. "He's trying to be something he's not. I think he hates the sea, the navy, everything he's doing. His wife's father was an admiral. You'd never guess it unless you thought about those eyebrows, but his own father was a Baptist minister."

"Are you Catholic?"

"Catholic? What the hell's that got to do with it? Yes, I'm catholic, a Jew with a classical education and a nigger heart. I'd make a good pope. Would you like to hear how I met him?"

"Who?"

"I had a pupil once who wanted to be a good sailor, but was deathly afraid of water. One day, to get over his fear, he decided all by himself to take a small boat out in what later turned out to be one of the worst storms of that year. He got over his fear. He got over his life. His father, who I knew was an Annapolis man, came down . . ."

"You mean you think Hake is doing the same thing?"

Dolfus let out his breath, relaxed back in his chair. He seemed deflated. "Yes, I guess that's what I mean," he said slowly.

"Go on. I didn't mean to interrupt you."

Dolfus shook his head. "It doesn't matter. You've got the important part. I'm tired of talking."

After a while Dolfus broke the silence. "We better go back and see if we can help the poor unhappy prick." He rose and began folding the deck chair, shaking his head. "Christ, I feel sorry for any man as unhappy as that."

As they started up the ladder, one of the men joked after them: "Ah hear they brought in some fine poontang on that there cattle boat today, Lieutenant. Least, that what the man in the goodcheer gallery say."

"It'll still be there tomorrow, Clarence. You pass your second class and you can watch them get off the boat. Don't forget to count the tools before you secure."

"They'll be there tomorrow if they aren't all used up tonight," one of the other men said, laughing.

"Get your wife to complain to your congressman, Dukes."

The other men hooted and laughed around Dukes and the noises of horseplay followed Sulgrave up over the top of the ladder.

They discussed the funeral, she explaining all through dinner who the people were who attended—it amounted to a brief history of her life with her husband. It was one of the best restaurants in Washington, and the food and service were good. They ate early, to be on time for the concert. Sulgrave listened as she talked, watching her closely whenever her eyes wandered to the people at other tables. "I hate the navy because it devoured him," she was saying, "but it wasn't the navy's fault. It takes two to make a feast, one who's hungry and one who wants to be eaten." Then she nodded toward a corner table. "I wonder why that woman is eating alone."

"Perhaps she owns the place," Sulgrave said lightly.

"She keeps looking toward the door as if she's expecting someone. I don't think she is."

And all through dinner, try as he would to keep track of her zigzagging conversation, one image kept floating through his mind: of her hand resting lightly on the dressing table to steady her balance, one sloped shoulder steeply below the other, as she reached down to change her shoes; of the black ribbon of silk that slipped delicately off her shoulder down her arm as she twisted the tight shoe on, breasts jiggling lightly. A warm ripe mystery of lace. A surge of life had struck through him then like a choir of hiccups.

Later in the evening, she confessed that she couldn't shake off the worry that she might have a chance meeting with one of their—her and her late husband's—service friends. She shied visibly every time she saw a naval uniform. They left the concert at the intermission and walked the chill distance back to her hotel. Sulgrave tried to ignore a vaguely shameful sense of anxiety mounting in him as they neared her hotel; it was too dangerous to admit, too profound to be cast off. He searched his mind for a better image of himself. She was only a few days a widow, a beautiful woman. Then, as though to placate conscience, forlorn angel of childhood, a shining gesture of righteousness broke through the dark swirl, like a sword from the lake: *Arrange for some flowers.* Flowers to brighten her room tomorrow—just the right thing. But no sooner had he grasped the blade of virtue than he perceived even in this pure act a delicate ambivalence of intent, felt the keen double edge. Tarnished by his own warm breath, the bright reflection clouded, and he returned from the future to the anxious present. They were nearing the hotel: *So what, I'll get her flowers anyway.*

At the hotel, just as he set the revolving doors in motion for her, she stopped and turned around. She faced him and tossed her white scarf back over her shoulder in a fluent gesture, and stood for a moment looking at him, both hands holding her fur coat closed tight under her chin.

She smiled at him. "Will you come up for breakfast?"

He laughed lightly, gave the revolving door another push, more dilatory. "I'd be delighted, although at this time of night I'd rather have a drink."

On that brief pinnacle of time he halted, suspended, stopped by her look. From her immediate eyebrow he sensed he'd blundered, overshot. He felt the smile sticking to his face like adhesive plaster—the hush-thumping revolving doors slowed to a whisper and glided to a mocking stop—her smile just barely hardened, not enough for him to be certain of what she felt. *Come up? She said come up.* She said noth-

125

ing, did nothing, made no clear move that would help him hatch his uncertainty. *Meant tomorrow?*

"Perhaps," he said lamely, "in the bar, before . . ."

"Your eagerness is flattering, Lieutenant." She said it coldly, suddenly.

For some reason he sensed relief; she had overstated it, as though she too were guilty of a thought crime. He felt easy again. He smiled, made a small bow. "Madame, I presume only to the modest possibility of a drink, nothing more."

The threat was momentarily past. She smiled. "That's not as flattering as I thought, then. A fledgling widow needs all the flattery she can get." She held out her hand decisively. "You can have your drink tomorrow—for breakfast. I've had a lovely time."

He shook her gloved hand. "It was my pleasure."

"Say around nine. I'd like to go shopping early. Would you like to come with me?"

"I have two weeks of leave. All of it is at your service."

"You're very sweet. Tomorrow, then." She turned and was gone, waving a gloved kiss through the turning glass panel.

As Sulgrave walked through the last night of November back to his own room at the Mayflower, he felt peculiarly empty; the mood of keyed attention was gone. As he picked up his key at the desk, he paused a moment and looked at it in his hand and had a suffocating vision of his anonymous room upstairs. It seemed aimless to take the elevator up. Suddenly he was struck with a loneliness so acute as to be almost a wrath; it seemed like a delayed reaction to the funeral, since that was what he found himself suddenly thinking about. Then he thought of the broken sword in his suitcase upstairs; the steam heat would be stifling. . . .

He broke off thinking, pocketed his key, headed for the

street. Again a fleeting remembered image: of Vanna again, of her straightening up and catching him staring at her, a momentary sharp question in her eyes; and the eloquence of a woman's common gesture: the hitching of her shoulder strap back into place with a hooked thumb. A womanly rap on the knuckles.

(Unsure of the room number, she hesitates before the door, searches her purse for the key she already holds in her left hand, discovers it, compares the brown fiberboard tag with the number on the door before her. The room is hers. As she inserts the key, her attention is arrested by the fact that her hand is shaking. She enters, closes the door behind her and leans back against it, pulls jerkily at her gloves finger by finger.)

that's right   stand up   refuse the blindfold
damned gloves   then why wear them
why can't you learn
what you need   what you want   *why lie*
nerves rubbed raw   *oh no more no more no no*
oh Lord I refuse to take a pill again
fool puritan bitch

(She removes her coat, tucks the white scarf into the sleeve, drops it over a chair, catches her reflection in a mirror opposite, halts.)

all right   I admit

                                         He's young
self-possessed   *afraid he'd run*
   afraid he'd fail you   *true*
expose you   *true*
   damn him   so young unneedful
   afraid he'd refuse   say no   *or laugh*
what is the truth   *admit the truth*
   afraid he'd be tactful   I don't want to beg
true or false   *beggar beggar*

you have no choice scairdy cat   you're alone
   All past   all past now
   I'm a woman   I must be my own woman
   But 38   God how will I get through
the night without going crazy   *no pill no pill*
   I'll go crazy if I don't sleep
get undressed anyway   God look at your hollow eyes
you're an old woman   He's made you see
made you see through his eyes
   Get undressed
   See through his eyes
   Get undressed
   (She moves aimlessly around the sitting room undoing her
dress and unfastening her pearls, her gaze glancing from one
object to another as though studying the texture of her sur-
roundings. Absently she goes into the bedroom dropping
clothing wherever it comes off, enters the bathroom wearing
girdle, stockings, shoes. She opens both taps and stands idly
before the sink with the water running, gazing again at her
reflection in the mirror.)

The record came to the end again; the needle slipped into the endless off-center groove and oscillated back and forth in the scratchy silence. Nobody moved to shut it off.

But the Commander wasn't asleep yet. He raised his head from his arms and glared blear-eyed across the desk into space. "Steward!" He lurched forward slightly as his folded arms slipped on the desk top. Orval BlueEyes scuttled in from the veranda and went straight to the phonograph. He was wearing a white mess jacket. He lifted the needle and started vigorously to wind the crank again. Hake turned his head and focused his eyes with effort on Orval. "Theah you are," he said in a minstrel-show accent, "you shif'less black good-f'-nothin'. Put it on again. Keep on playin' it till Ah tell you t' stop. I want these gemmun to hear mah fav'rit song with me."

Hake swung his head toward Dolfus, who was sitting profiled on one window ledge, then to Sulgrave, sitting opposite on the other. "An', Steward, refresh the gemmun's drinks. I don't wan' t' keep havin' to ask yuh."

Orval continued to crank. No one said anything. Both Dolfus and Sulgrave had full drinks in plain view. Hake's was empty. He reached for the bottle at his elbow, splashed into his glass. "Rum ssa sailor's drink. Bourbon or rum. Anythin' else is for gemmun an' the ladies." He took a half lime from the bowl in front of him, mashed it between his fingers and palm and dropped it into the glass. "Keep y' teeth from fallin' out." Then he dumped a spoonful of powdered sugar in and stirred it sloppily with the same spoon. The desk top was a sticky mess of spilled liquor and powdered sugar. "Energy," he said.

"Steward! More ice!"

"Ain't no more ice, suh. We ran out a long time ago."

Hake grunted. "Damn kerosene icebox." Then he looked at Dolfus, whose head was turned toward the calm black sea. "Making ice with fire. Thas' something to think 'bout. You think 'bout it."

The needle went into the groove, hissing loudly. Then the first tinny notes of ragtime banjo issued from the machine, and the cymbal-shot that was the starting gun for the rest of the band: rick, rick-tickety-too. . .

> Oh, you beau-ti-ful doll,
> You great big beau-ti-ful doll . . .

Dolfus grimaced and took a sip from his glass. Sulgrave watched him. This was the twentieth time the record had been played since they arrived. How many times before that, and on how many other nights before this night, was impossible to guess. But to Sulgrave's ear the record was almost worn through to the other side; the lyrics were nearly incomprehensible under the scratching of the cactus needle. Hake took a long pull on his drink, and dropped his head over his folded arms again.

It was after midnight by Sulgrave's watch, and he was tiring of the vigil. He wasn't quite sure what they were waiting for, since apparently Hake had already had at least one fit of rage before they arrived. The girl was gone—if for certain she had ever been there. Bored, Sulgrave swung one leg out over the window ledge, straddling it like a horse.

The place had been a shambles when they first came in; one of the bookcases had been pulled over, and Orval was busy replacing the spill of volumes. The Commander was then in his bedroom. When Orval went in to announce their arrival, Hake had come out carrying the phonograph. It was playing even then "Oh, You Beautiful Doll," with the needle yawing back and forth over the grooves as Hake lurched into the room. Orval took the machine and set it up on top of the bookcase.

Hake was full of overinsistent joviality, a sort of deadly mixture of drunken boisterousness with a truculent determination to prove it. They were just in time to join the party. This was the party.

Sulgrave had by now drunk just enough to feel pleasantly warm. He watched the comatose Hake behind his kneehole desk, and felt certain that it wouldn't be long before he failed to notice when the music stopped. From there it would be a simple matter to get him to bed. The bottle on the desk was nearly empty. Orval had gone back to the veranda, where Sulgrave could just make out the outlines of his white jacket in the darkness; he would be sitting on the top step with Big Randy, silently sipping beer, waiting.

As the record was about to end again, Orval came in, put it on from the beginning. Dolfus yawned and looked at his watch, cast a bored, expressionless glance at Sulgrave, then at Hake, shrugged, and looked out the window again.

Then it happened. Hake slowly sat up, stared for a moment as though astounded, then jumped up and bellowed a curse. *"Hard right! Full astern! God damn you, you hear me?"* Dolfus put down his glass and swung his legs to the floor.

Sulgrave was so surprised at the force of the voice that in trying to get his leg back inside he lost his balance and fell backward out the window. A few feet below, he lay on his back gazing at the moon, hearing music. He disentangled himself from the bushes and stood up just in time to see: Orval gaping, undoubtedly wondering what the Lieutenant was doing looking in the window; and Dolfus, despite everything, holding his sides laughing.

Then, like a magic-lantern slide, the scene changed again. "*Sabotage!*" Hake shouted. "Get every one those black devils out on deck. Port and starboard watches. Get 'em out. Wake them up. Turn them out! I'll get them out myself . . ."

With that he lifted one side of the heavy desk and turned it onto the floor with a horrendous crash. Bottle, glass, sugar bowl, tray—everything went skittering. Orval ran across to help Sulgrave climb back in the window and went down on a wet lime, windmilling backwards as his feet scuttled out from under him. The falling desk had so jarred the frail room that the phonograph needle rasped across the disc, and was just starting over from the beginning when Orval's less ponderous thump kicked it out of its groove and started it again.

> Oh, you beau-ti-ful doll,
> You great big beau-ti-ful . . . zzzxk . . .
>
> Oh, you beau-ti-ful doll . . .

"*Start the pumps!*" Hake shouted. "Bridge to Damage Control—check bilges for water!"

Hake hadn't budged from where he was standing. He stood glassy-eyed amid the chaos around him, weaving slightly and shouting into empty air, his face purple, eyebrows twitching. Dolfus wasn't doing anything yet, but looked ready for whatever might come. Orval picked himself up off the floor. The phonograph continued to spill its cackling lyric out into the starry night.

Insanity.

Then the scene changed again. Hake saw Orval, shouted, "Conspiring to break a lawful command. The whole lot of them." He pulled free a drawer from the desk and raised it over his head, scattering papers all over the room. "A good flogging, that's what . . ."

Before he could heave the drawer, Dolfus snatched it out of his hand, but Orval was still ducked to a running crouch when he collided with Big Randy coming in the door. Hake swept Dolfus aside with one powerful sweep of his arm; Dolfus and the empty drawer were slammed hard against the wall; the bungalow boomed like a drum. Zzzxk! For a suspended instant there was utter silence. Nothing moved. Then came the ragtime banjo, the cymbal-shot, and the music started again, from the beginning.

Oh, you beau-ti-ful doll . . .

The Commander had just started around the desk toward the door blocked by Big Randy, when Sulgrave gave up his frantic effort to hoist himself in by the window and started around toward the door on the veranda. As he ran past the window fronting Orval's vegetable garden, he tripped on the wire supporting the string-bean vines and went down. Getting up he glanced in the window for an instant and saw Randy and the Commander swaying in a static embrace and looking for all the world as though they were dancing to the idiot music. But as Sulgrave came around the corner of the veranda, there was an enormous shuffling of feet and a crash as heavy bodies collided with the near wall. Sulgrave heard the boards crunch. Orval flew out the door and off the top step in one bound, his white jacket flapping like a night bird into the gloom, stopped, ran back up the steps to look in. As Sulgrave creaked up the steps behind him, there was total silence inside. Then, inevitably, but this time as though sick from fatigue, the Commander's favorite song began again, winding down from the beginning; and Sulgrave knew that whatever was going to happen, had happened. The Commander's party was over for tonight.

Oh

    you

        beautiful

            doll

Y
 o
  u

     g
      r
       e
        a
         t

         b
          i
           g

            b
             e
              e
               o
                o

Widow   How like a schoolgirl
   Look at you
                    Trying to feel sorry
wanting to weep   feel genuine   *nothing*
   Emptyhanded widow   *alone*
false face false feelings   *twist twist*
even have to try to cry
   Look at you   look at
   Are you satisfied   happy with yourself
   This
   Is this what you wanted   *alone*
alone in the state you're in
   is it
   dreary horrid room   alone
   Is this what you made a fool of
myself for
   to have his company for dinner
just to come back to an empty room
and stare at this face in this mirror
                              empty room empty bed
trying to cry in front of yourself
   been alone before
alone all your life   *please not now not*
no time to be alone   no one should
   I want to feel decent
   I can't feel he's really dead
that he's really dead what does that mean
can't get it through this head that he's

really dead   *nothing's changing*
   except
   terrible feeling   awful
   I'm sick of you   me
of not feeling clean   being false   sick
of not hurting   only wanting him
   wanting who   *not true*
   only wanting   *shame shame*
but I can't have him now or before

                                   oh hateful

   What is *this* feeling
something terrible will happen to me
   Something terrible is going to happen
something is going to happen to me
   what is this feeling   *room room*
why   what am I so afraid of   *I am I am I*
   sorry he's dead   *yesyesyesyesyes*
   properly sorry   *oh please*
   O Jesus I don't know how to feel
I don't feel right don't feel the way I should
want to feel sorry but all I feel is afraid
sorry I was so rotten to him sorry he loved
   something terrible
   I'm going to die   that's what
it makes me know I'm going to die
           me know I'm going to die alone
   I did my best   I tried
   Oh God   My best   *fool blind*
like I did my best tonight   my lieutenant
best   my leveling best   *cry cry*
   I make them all miserable   all all
miserable   I used to hate it when they tried
to look down my front   because I knew what

they were feeling   even as a girl I loved
to look at them and I knew what they were
   feeling
   Red marks   ugly elastic
               Oh God our Father oh please Forgiver
   He was a miserable man   he was
unhappy when I married him   even before
but I knew it   wanted to make him happy
he didn't want me following him didn't want
me   not with him   *not the whole truth*
   That was only after
   Before   I went with him everywhere
   loved him loved him   even if I'm
forcing tears   false tears   please let me cry
   loved him   it's true true
oh it was true was true was true
   What happened   try to cry   to feel
what happened   I loved him
   what happened
   I can't feel sorry because I can't feel
Even when I saw that damned horrid box they
brought him home in with the flag over it
even then   said to yourself like a question
   he's dead
   trying on the feeling to see how it fit
   Cry   go on cry   *oh please let*
   didn't fit
   and hated going out to buy a black dress
to mourn him   hate black   trying on a feeling
to see what it does for you   rotten little hypocrite
   There   at last
   Cry   oh let it come
   cry cry cry cry cry

oh come   more more more   thank
  Oh God   you took so long to come
he was always away from me always off somewhere
explosion whole island a disaster should I go
see where it happened know what happened feel
what happened need to feel it need to feel
need to feel something anything that's real
sorry for him because he was alone and alone
he needed more time more love and more time
I couldn't give to him always felt alone with
him   *Oh God God God*
please please I'm still all alone alone
help me
oh help me   ss
                                    srry
                               sorry fr

    Sorry for yourself not him you
mean more love than he could give you
you can cry but you can't clean out
the rottenness inside   *inside inside*
so empty you ache
    Why can't you feel decent feelings
stiff old father cried without trying and
cried for three days while she was dying
all you could do was hate him
                       do was hate him so he died
    Oh God God I'm going down on my knees
    I'm going down on my knees to you
    hated hated for not letting you wear
lipstick and silk stockings and for trying to
bring you me up a decent woman
                  a decent woman he loved more
                         like her

he cried for her   I think yes   not him
    Please God please please
    I give up I give in   I loved him
I loved him for everything   I give up give up
    Oh damn God if you died without knowing
    I'm sorry God I repent bite my tongue
is there God anywhere any more   then why is this
me   *Oh please Forgiver*
I'm all alone
    Daddy daddy I really loved you I didn't
know I was spoiled I was rotten I was rotten and
she died and I'm sorry sorry sorry for being sorry
listen listen to her listen to him in there with
her crying over her and I with my ear this very
ear against that bedroom door listening and hating
and I didn't even know she was that sick and dying
hating him for making noise and sniveling over her
because she was sick and upsetting her   *liar lie*
yes yes I kept the lipstick even after I promised
him
    Someone   Someone please forgive me
please please   someone or God or anybody
    Look I'm sorry
    this crying is real   listen look at me
sorry because it's always too late to be sorry
tears fine rich tears alone and great loosening
too late to be forgiven   *wallowing*
can't be anything else but sorry   cry out of
hope cry for a witness   cry for a forgiver
I was never sorry when I was forgiven I did
what I pleased. He was right you're not decent
    you're sorry for yourself
    No way out of the circle

Hell   get up off your knees
the tile is cold
    Knees hurt
    And you thought of your stockings first
didn't you   went down carefully so you wouldn't
snag them   more than just crossed your mind
admit it   admit admit   can't even pray
without
    have another pair in the blue vanity case
forgot   so terrible   Am I to blame for every
stray thought   oh hell I know it   *too late too*
mind's crossed
    Think what you're thinking now
thinking on my knees over a toilet bowl like a drunk
I'm not even aware   *vomiting drunk*
    Staring
    Tiles   white tiles   millions of tiles
thousands of bathrooms   hundreds of times sitting
small white tiles
    Octagons   no   one two three makes half
other half makes six
    Hexagon
    All right   I'm alone   all right all
right all right   got what I deserve   *oh true*
Isn't that punishment enough
    Get up fool   you wouldn't want to wear it
but you did
    Didn't want a girdle to encase me
                                In case he in case we
Admit it again   planned on having him
    didn't want to put anything in his way
make it easy   *fallen drunk vomiting*
    Don't make it worse

141

Get up   hypocrite

fallen fallen

Get up woman   aging flirt
Get up and use the toilet for what it was made for
take it off now   and your precious silk hose
flab
Really need to go   not an excuse

Our Father

I'm not a hypocrite
never kill myself   when did I go last
before dinner no wonder
have so much
Not like a young girl any more
sound like an old horse   randy mare in spring
only thing only insult he ever said I liked
only insult I really loved   *young*
38   the wheels keep turning
God I'll go crazy here tonight by myself
Why are you letting the water run
turn it off   get up go to bed   God look at you
old woman   must seem how through his eyes
Try to go to bed anyway   *Our Father*
Try to see
Go to bed   *who art*
pick up the room   no   *in Heaven hal*
Vannessa Lee Lynch   *low*
Look in the big mirror   *ed*
Woman goes berserk   *be*
Hake   *Our Father*
I'm not a hypocrite   I'm by myself
Looking out the window before seven floors
hitting the street   smash   hitting God head on
Woman in nightgown   no girdle   would we leave note

No note
           big X on girdle found in room
Big X in lipstick
Outrage
Lady thrown from wild party   you take her head
I'll take her feet   one two three heave-ho
Daddy Daddy
Oh why

Sulgrave had the duty Sunday, and the day passed hot and still without incident. Nothing broke the witless blue calm. The shutters of the Commander's quarters remained closed until late afternoon, with Orval coming in and out ministering to household needs as though nothing had happened. Nothing else stirred in the muffling heat. Sulgrave took a swim before sundown, ate dinner by himself, and went to bed early. He hadn't seen Dolfus since they had walked down from the Commander's after helping Orval put him to bed. Dolfus said good night, said he wanted to take a walk. Sulgrave looked in Dolfus' room in the morning; his bed hadn't been slept in.

Sulgrave was awakened at dawn Monday by someone lightly touching his shoulder; for a confused instant he thought he was dreaming. He sat up, looked at his watch, then back at Arielle. She stood silently watching him, her eyes round in the early sunless gloom of the room. He opened a louver and peered at the sky; it couldn't have been much after sunrise.

"What is it?" he asked, rubbing his eyes. He stared at the girl. She didn't answer.

"What's the matter?"

"Can't find Randy," she said. "Skully won't wake up."

At first he thought it was an accident, and as he pulled on his clothes, had visions of Dolfus lying unconscious somewhere—a fall or something.

But it wasn't an accident. Leaving the operations area, he quizzed the girl as he walked beside her toward the cut; Dolfus was passed out. "He drink a lot. I never see him sleep so hard. He say never let him sleep past muster time. So I came to get Randy, but he not there. Get you."

She had a curious singsong way of talking, as though her mother tongue were French. Dolfus had said her father was Spanish.

"You speak French?" he asked.

"Si," she said.

She had her own shallop, and she crossed the cut alone. Sulgrave didn't bother starting the outboard since the current was slack, but simply poled across. She was waiting for him when he reached the other side.

From that point, she took him by the hand and led him. Her hand was cool and very narrow; she was completely unconscious of Sulgrave studying her as they walked. Her hair was long and glossy blue-black, her cheeks high, her skin mocha. She walked with barefooted grace; the one-piece cotton dress was all she wore. She led him toward the shack near the laundry, where he'd first seen her the first day.

"Can you make coffee?"

She nodded.

"Who's in there?" he asked, nodding to the back room. A curtain was closed across the doorway, but someone else was snoring besides Dolfus.

"Old Woman and Girlchild," she said.

The stove was in a lean-to in the yard. She took the pot and a coffee can under her arm and went out.

The tiny building was raised on posts, and divided by a middle partition into two rooms. He found Skully on a canvas cot in the first room; his uniform hung over his head from a cross beam. He was wearing a faded sport shirt with all the buttons gone, blue slacks, and he was out cold, snoring dead to the world. The bottoms of his feet were black from going barefoot.

Sulgrave felt edgy and nervous from lack of sleep as he paced the block in front of Vanna's hotel waiting for his watch to make the right angle at nine. He had been the last person out of the Mayflower bar when it closed in the small hours, and had walked again for half an hour before going up to his room. There he'd lain awake the remaining hours unable to sleep, his mind turning over a tumult of thoughts and images like a waking nightmare: of Hake, and Dolfus, both dead; of the child-woman Arielle, gone where?; of the funeral, and the men; of Vanna, and again Vanna, and yet again Vanna. At one point he jumped from bed determined to destroy the letters in the red leather box at the bottom of his suitcase. Instead he sat down on the bed and guiltily read them again, feeling unaccountably angry now, even jealous. Disgusted with himself, he stuffed them back into their box and buried it beneath his shirts again. And the sword that had belonged to her father, then to her husband—surely a skillful craftsman could restore it for service in a museum case: why hadn't he told her about that either? The truth was he knew he wanted to keep it, broken or not.

When the sky lightened toward dawn, he was actually glad for the reprieve from darkness, more glad to get up. He dressed and went out, ate breakfast in an all-night cafeteria where an old man was mopping the floor to start the day. Then he walked in the park, watched an old woman feeding pigeons—apparently her daily ritual, since she had hundreds of them cooing about her feet as she scattered bread crumbs. He noticed that whenever she could, she threw something for the sparrows, who tended to get shouldered to the periphery of the cooing and weaving mass.

"Man, whut *you* think?"

"What do I think about what? I'm tryin' to get done some readin'."

"Man, put you' book down and listen to whut the cat sayin'. He telling me all this shit 'bout the sun coolin' down and the fire goin' out and we all gone be left freezin' ouah asses off."

"I don't say right away. It goin' to take time. You all be long gone when it happens. Millions of years gone."

"What do you want me to say?"

"Do you believe in that?"

"I don't know but what the Book say. The Book say the world goin' end by fire."

"You show me where it say that. I looked all through it and couldn't find it once. Sunday school teacher couldn't find it neither."

"What happened?"

"Tole me to hush my mouth and not be so smart. But I don' believe it in there."

"That's what I don't believe either. Sun's goin' to cool down, I tell you."

"Man, you cats always arguin'. Whyn't you argue some place else? Get some peace and quiet around this barracks."

"Man, don't you *never* stop reading?"

"I ain't got time to spend worryin' about where the world's goin'. I'm too busy worryin' 'bout where *I'm* goin. Because *when* you gone, you a *long* time gone. What else you want to know?"

At eight, he had found a florist opening and had ordered flowers to be delivered to Vanna's hotel later that morning; he left their choice up to the woman in the store, explaining only that they should be "cheerful." It was chilly outside, and after ordering the flowers, he had three more cups of coffee in that many different places as he killed time before nine o'clock. When finally he turned on his heel and headed for the revolving door, he was as tense as a drawn bowstring.

He went up in the elevator without announcing himself at the desk, his mind a witless blank as he found his way through the corridor to her room; the door was ajar. He knocked, heard her call Come in—from deep inside.

She was sitting up in bed propped with pillows, a news-paper lying discarded on the covers, a breakfast tray on the floor beside her. He took off his coat in the doorway.

"I was so hungry I couldn't wait," she said. "I had break-fast hours ago. How'd you sleep?"

He hardly trusted himself to speak—he just grunted, shook his head negatively.

"Come here, let me look at you." She examined his face narrowly. "You look terrible. Sit down."

He sat down on the bed, the paper slid off onto the floor.

"I didn't sleep much either," she admitted. "It was the funeral, and all the strain. I couldn't stop thinking about it."

She looked drawn and tired, and to Sulgrave all the more beautiful. She had very little makeup on; what she wore she had applied with care. Her face was tired, but her hair had been brushed till it shone in the light that poured in the window. The nightgown, or whatever the thing was she was wearing, was white froth shot with ivory lace. Her shoulders and arms were bare, only partly covered by a bed jacket of pale blue silk.

He couldn't stop looking at her; passively she stared back. Looking at his face, she seemed to see that there was little need for pretense, and gradually her carefully prepared countenance changed from false cheerfulness to the geunine strain she was feeling.

"The only decent moment of the whole day was when I fell asleep in the car. I'm just beginning to realize what it means to be thirty-eight," she said. "I don't have the emotional stamina I used to. I don't bounce back as I did when I was your age. It's harder to break out of old forms, to find new life. To resurrect yourself when part of yourself has died."

"I'm not so young as you think, then."

"I've never seen before how young you really are," she said. "Last night you were the gallant and handsome squire. This morning you've changed. If you look younger, I must look older than ever."

"You're beautiful."

"You're very kind." She said it coldly, looked down at her hands, her mouth hardened to a line. Her face was peculiarly strained, almost as though she were about to scream or break into tears. The last layer of pretense was falling away; beneath the mask showed the real state of anguish in which she had passed the night. Her disguises were crumbling so fast that it was bewildering. "I wonder what you'd think if you really knew me, if you saw all of me."

"I didn't say that to be kind. You *are* beautiful. You're one of the most beautiful women I've ever seen. It's not a compliment. It's just the plain truth." He was baffled, panicked at having offended her.

She looked at him unbelievingly. He almost wanted to look away from her gaze, as gradually her face took on again the same peculiar look of intense tension. She looked at him as though any second she might, might—he didn't know what. There was a long strained silence as she searched his face, for what? For the truth? He saw one thing clearly in her eyes: fear. Suddenly she wrung her hands once, and leaned forward, pleaded with him, "What must I do? Please *tell* me, what must I *do?*"

"Why do you have to do anything? This is no time to try to decide anything. How can you even *think* after a night with no sleep?"

"What do I have to *do?*" Even her eyes were beseeching. "I *need* you."

He shrugged defensively, suddenly alerted to an electric situation; it was something in her tone, the strange hollowness. Suddenly she lay back and relaxed against the stacked pillows, oddly calm. No words were adequate to the sensation he felt in his stomach; something was going to happen. Then he realized that he himself must look the same way she did, falsely calm; he had been unconsciously controlling his face to offset her edging hysteria. The tension between them was like a tuned wire. How could all this have happened in just the few minutes he'd been here?

"All right," she said, coldly exasperated.

For a full minute, time passed like water dripping on a rain puddle, each moment expanding outward in the senses in slow rings. He stared at her, sensing every movement of flesh, every tremor of muscle—his own and hers—as though the slow flutter deep in his gut were hers, *was* her. He saw the pulse beat of her throat, almost heard the irregular rise and fall of her breasts. He felt strung to the point of vague nausea—too much coffee, no sleep, tension of undreamt dreams: all of it was nothing to the tension she was creating in him by looking at him in that deadly calm way. One shoulder was no longer under the jacket.

As each of them came to terms with the silent tension, its nature became inescapable, clear. Her face relaxed, was no longer so grimly calm, but merely expressionless. Only her slight breathing betrayed her.

She spoke so softly that her voice was almost a dry whisper. "I didn't want to be the one responsible," she said. "I've wanted you all night. I almost called you."

He understood her, understood exactly his own failure to act, even his incapacity to act now. He could think of nothing to say, no way to close the terrible distance still between them, except to lunge at her so she wouldn't see his face. But a failure of courage seemed better than a failure of grace, although he knew he'd already failed her in both. As for his failure of himself, he felt completely at sea, like an adolescent before the mysteries. He simply nodded his admission.

"Would you like to look at me?" Her voice was very soft, hollow with excitement, yet curiously gentle, almost contrite.

In the pale silence the question beat in his ears, its thick meaning almost overwhelming. Uncertain, he was almost unwilling to speak. He barely nodded.

Without taking her eyes off his face, she very slowly pulled the bed jacket off her shoulders and dropped it off the bed to the floor, then paused, watching him. He gazed at her naked shoulders, at the ripeness of her, guessed wildly at her breasts still hidden.

The look in her eyes was peculiarly flat, lusterless, her face still without expression as she raised her hands and searched in the lace of her bodice until she found the hook and eye and first hidden button. She unbuttoned it with perfect deliberation; dropped her fingers to the next; undid it; then down to the next—all the time gazing at his face unblinkingly with that flat, distant look in her eyes.

She proceeded with careful precision from the first button to the next, over the nice curve of herself, and down to her waist, and stopped. She paused again, examining his face before going on. A tiny river of naked flesh ran up from her waist to the delta below her neck; she tilted her chin up in a minuscule gesture and light caught her eyes, suddenly brought them alive. She sat for a moment with her hands in her lap.

Then, measuring his reaction, she raised her hands, caught the lace front in both hands and arched her back. Smoothly, as though opening a stage curtain, she spread wide the opening of her gown and exposed her nipples erect to his stare. The pulled straps slipped off her shoulders one at a time.

He sat looking at her, at this splendor before him, and felt almost paralyzed with incomprehensible relief, dark rejoicing of his flesh.

Suddenly she threw back the covers, and in a naked flash of legs was out of bed, naked to the waist. She moved toward the full-length mirror on the bathroom door, and turned before it like a dancer watching herself. Then she walked halfway toward him, stopped, gazing at him as though from a dream. Undoing the last few buttons, she worked the gown off her hips and let it slide to the floor. Suddenly she giggled. The mysterious dark shock was like a hammer blow on his senses. Paralysis gave way like a dam cracking, and he was on his feet undressing for joy and good fortune. A moment later he was naked as a hat rack and went down laughing on the bed with her, laughing like a madman.

Yessum

Ringleader

no use I'm in it now. That man gone, all the way gone. If you white you right, even crazy white.

you brown get down

black get back

I'm too late to get back this time, too late and too old. Big Randolph, you on to be a biggity nigger for sure this time

Mutiny. Leastwise Brother Boy ain't sittin' here, kept him straight leastwise. He got to keep up learnin' to type

Tell Skully, ask him

Black man, you in one helpless fix. Ain't doing no one no good here, can't even look out for last blood kin

should know better to fool with a ofay crazy man

White-crazy. Man, figger bigger, nigger.

Man, listen to ol' Digger snore. Must be dreamin'

Some white officer chasin' him with a sword, that wild sword. Can't even figger what goes in the head of a man like that to make him so twisted up

like an ol' swamp root, used to think they were snakes sometimes. Ghosts at night. Ghosts are white, son, be proud you black.

You gotta look after him, you promised her. Help him learn something keep him out of trouble ask the Lord for guidance

Yessum

Don't want you and him dying in a shack like me, get him out, Randolph. Come him up in the world. Go north and provide

Yessum

". . . afraid to let him touch me. Finally he courted me so . . ."

"Did he love you then?"

". . . well, I married him, and after that I thought it would be easy to have it, but when you've been years building up the idea that something is wrong and sinful, just because you're married doesn't change what you've taught yourself and so it took time. I hadn't had much experience with how awful things like that can be, but I lied to you when I told you before that I was a virgin for him. I told him I was because it seemed too terribly important to him and actually I was, except physically. It was a terrible lie for me, and I had to make myself believe it before I could tell it—I can't explain more than that. You're the first person I've even told, not even my doctor, not another soul, not even . . . I'm telling you because it shouldn't matter now. Because even after I knew he was dead I kept thinking that I had never been unfaithful to him until after Sevie's death, until then when you asked me and it was like being forced into remembering something I'd forgotten. I knew of course, only I've been pretending for so long that I guess I really didn't know any more or almost *had* forgotten. He married me because I was an ideal for him, everything he wanted to be himself. He wanted me to stay on a pedestal. Yes, he loved me then. But I married him because he was everything I wanted and needed, or so I thought. He was rough. When I first met him I was only fourteen and he was one of the officers on the base at Norfolk. Four years later when my father was at the Academy, he came to the house to make his duty call and six months later we were married. Daddy hated him almost from the start, I think because he saw that he was trying to be something he wasn't. He was trying to be an officer and a gentleman. As an officer, he was brilliant, even the Old Admiral, Daddy, admitted that—he was forty-one when I was born, Mother said they had given up hope of having children. But as a gentleman, in those days he wasn't as polished as he was by the time you knew him. His father was a Baptist preacher in a West Virginia coal town, a part-time miner on weekdays. He was ashamed of his father and his background, but couldn't admit it to himself. He looked just like his father. His father once saved the life of a miner who later became a power in the union and got Severn a congressional appointment to the Academy. He always used the name Severn because it sounded more gentlemanly than Bonuso, which was the name of his mother's father. His mother was dead when I married him and I could never get much out of him about her family. To him I was everything that she hadn't been. But after we were married, instead of relaxing and being himself, he got worse. And in his eyes I got worse too. He once called me a slut because I wanted to leave a party and go home and make love. It took nearly a year before I could have one every time, but after it first happened I wanted to keep at it for fear I'd lose it. I was sure it was a matter of practice and I tried very hard—not to please him but to please myself. He couldn't understand I was just becoming a woman. He wanted me to be a lady. Well, I'm not a lady—I married him to escape being a lady I suppose. But little by little he managed to kill the things in himself that had attracted me to him—the rough earthy things that made him a man to me. And when our son was born everything went wrong from the start. He wouldn't let me pick him up when

155

he was crying for fear I'd spoil him, but I guess I spoiled him anyway. I don't know. He didn't want to go to Annapolis. He didn't like football and rowing. He liked to read and collect things from the time he was a little boy, and I suppose I encouraged him. Perhaps it was wrong of me, I don't know. I don't know. I remember once when he was nine, he had a collection of seashells—he never went in the water, just walked along the beach looking for shells—and his father gave them away when he went off to school in the fall. He said he was spending too much time indoors, poring over them, putting them in glass frames with cotton under them. He was very serious, knew all the Latin names for them. And they *were* beautiful. I blame myself terribly for . . . I never knew how to take his part without infuriating his father. There was a terrible scene when he came home for Thanksgiving and found the shells gone. His father was away at sea, and I was alone. Perhaps I was wrong, but I bought him another collection from a dealer and gave it to him for Christmas. But he hardly ever looked at the shells after that. I still have the collection in the attic in Annapolis. After his death I couldn't look at them without crying. It was after that—I feel I want to tell you everything, although I can't help feeling like a betrayer even though he's dead—it was after the death of our son that the marriage seemed to fail . . . Severn blamed himself, but secretly I think he blamed me. At any rate, he changed. He went back to duty and left me alone to blame myself, and that was why I went to see Ben Dolfus one day. He was the only person who had ever shown any interest in the child—I guess he was no longer a child if he was at prep school. Perhaps it's true that I didn't want to see him become a man, but I think that is an unfair accusation. I wanted him to grow up, but in his own way. But after that nothing was the same. Severn still wanted me as a woman, but it got worse and worse. When he was home, bedtime became something we both learned to put off —or I'd go to bed and he would stay up reading. At first it was never out in the open, because when we came home from a party where we'd been drinking then it would be all right. Then we began having a few drinks at home, nightcaps more or less—we still hadn't discussed it openly, it was all unspoken as though if we ignored it it wouldn't be a problem. He began to drink more and more—it seemed to be the only way he could relax and be himself. But finally even that failed— he would drink so much that it was worse than if he hadn't had anything. He ascribed it to age, but it wasn't age, it was something in him that was eating at him. All during this time —especially during Christmas holidays and such, when he was home and school was adjourned—we were seeing Ben socially. Severn liked Ben immensely and tried to help him. They would stay up talking half the night over brandy—history, politics, literature, mathematics, I don't know what all. I've told myself so many lies about this that I can't remember which lies I've told you. But the truth is that Ben and I didn't want to carry on an affair—we both felt it was terribly wrong. After those first times, I didn't see him for nearly a year. It was Severn who brought us together again by insisting that we 'owed' something of ourselves to Lieutenant Dolfus for having been kind to . . . our son. I tried saying I didn't like him—that only infuriated my husband. He said I didn't really know him, and that I should make an effort. Well, I made an effort. We were terribly careful, but to this day I'm terrified at the thought that Severn suspected something. He had no reason to, but he seemed to go out of his way to throw us together, almost like an entrepreneur. I'm sure it's only my guilty imagination. In fact, I know it is. But I have to tell you—and I despise myself for this—when

157

they told me about the disaster, it never even occurred to me that Severn would be dead. For one thing I thought they would have told me that first, before they told me anything else. All I could think of was whether Ben had been hurt. But then when I found out that my husband was dead, too, suddenly it was all over. Ben's death simply vanished from my mind. It was as though he had never existed. How do you explain that? Please don't think me horrid for telling you this, but if I don't tell you the truth I'll never be able to tell myself the truth. Perhaps that's why I need you so desperately, to be my confessor more than my lover. I guess they're the same thing if you think about it. Ben was my one great sin, and I guess I was glad to forget it. I don't think we loved each other in any romantic way, it was a mutual need. But I always felt guilty, almost whorish. I was raised as a young puritan, and something like that stays with you until you're dead. I feel guilty being here with you right now. Rather I don't now, but I probably will. Yet I know that if I wasn't here with you, I'd probably be dead drunk, or maybe just dead. Or maybe with someone else. God. I wasn't made to be raised a puritan. I just wasn't made for it. The first man I kissed, I also . . . that was the time I meant. This is what I've really been trying to make myself tell you. Please be patient with me, because I've kept this inside me for twenty-two years. I was sixteen. The war was just over. I was stage-struck and used to sneak out of school to go to the theater matinées. I met a young ensign—Naval Reserve—he was about twenty, and he took me backstage to meet this actress who was in the play. It was very glamorous at the time. Then . . . Then . . . please try to understand. I know you'll say I'm being irrational, but if you can understand how I was brought up —no, don't nod your head, just listen and try to understand. I don't think so now, but then I knew that I caused my mother to die. You see, she had been ill but the doctors didn't think it was serious. But two weeks after that time, she caught influenza and died. Can you understand? I hardly knew where babies came from, and yet the first man to kiss me . . . I let him come inside me. I didn't even know what I was letting him do. It didn't even hurt me. No one had ever told me it was supposed to hurt. From the moment he put his hands on me I was too amazed and surprised at what I felt— I didn't want him to stop. He must have thought I was–I know he thought I wasn't a virgin–he told me later. And when he put his hand there I almost fainted from the sensation. I remember trying to speak–not to tell him to stop, but just to utter words–and I couldn't. I was paralyzed, a molten paralysis that I've never experienced before or since. I was frightened, yes, but only at the terrible strangeness of him, the moving around inside me, the feel of him against me. I don't think a man can even imagine how awesome he is to a young girl, the rough feel of him, and the smell. Mind you, I knew utterly nothing about sex. I didn't even know that I could become pregnant–it's hard for you to believe because you're younger and things are different today. But I didn't know until he said something about taking care of myself. I asked him what he meant, and he said, You don't want to be pregnant, do you? I almost died. The word pregnant was like a four-letter word in those days, at least in my family it was. The only thing that shocked me was his use of the word, not the act. I looked at him in terror and said, You mean I can have a baby from this? I'll never forget his face. You see, we were in a cornfield near the river–there's a State Department Building there now, I think–and I'd let him take all my clothes off. I'm not lying or making any of it up–I just didn't know anything–I had the idea that babies came from an operation of some kind that a doctor did, I guess from the association of babies and hospitals. But anyway, here I am, thirty-eight, and I still can't quite believe it myself. It's no wonder I later came to pretend it didn't happen. And two weeks later my mother died. I don't know why, but that's what I had to tell you."

Sulgrave sat crosslegged on the foot of the bed, naked, watching her as she lay back against the stacked pillows and reached for a cigarette. The match flame trembled very slightly as she lit it; she blew it out sharply, glanced at him.

"My hand betrays me," she said, sighing smoke.

"What happened to him?"

"Ah, the typical male question—what happened to *him*. Well, he was very young, not very experienced himself. He did what all young males do, talked very bravely about marriage until the panic had a few days to take root. I was certain my belly would swell any day. He left for Boston to be discharged—full of promises and resolves, which I'm perfectly sure he meant at the time. He wrote me. Several times. When finally I knew I wasn't pregnant—it took me a whole afternoon in the library with the Encyclopaedia Britannica to find out how you could tell—I wrote him and told him. Six months later I got a letter from England, where he had gone to resume his studies. Two years later he wrote me a letter that started out, I hope you will remember me from our meeting at the theater some years ago . . . He said he'd never forgotten me, as he was sure I had him, and that he was writing to tell me he was getting married to an English girl, an actress. It was a marriage that should have been mine, I felt, and I was beside myself with rage and heartbreak. I was even glad when I found out that she cuckolded him and wrecked his career in England. Got herself involved in a horrid scandal with a cabinet minister's son. Later he divorced her and came back here to forget. Instead of joining the foreign legion, he joined the Regular Navy, which in the twenties amounted to nearly the same thing I suppose. Unfortunately he loved her, never did forget her. He wasn't able."

"Did you ever see him again?"

"I wrote him when I got married."

"Then you never saw him after he left you?"

Vanna was silent a long moment. She sat reclined against the pillows and gazed at her outstretched legs as though unseeing of her own naked flesh, one hand limply halted in mid-gesture toward the ash tray on her belly. A ribbon of blue smoke twined up out of the spill of light from the bed lamp. Then she stubbed out the hardly consumed cigarette and put the ash tray aside.

"I . . ."

She hesitated again, this time drawing her legs up to her chest and hugging them, smoothing her cheeks against her knees. She rocked slightly back and forth a moment, then stopped, still hugging her knees, and looked directly into his eyes.

"You know who it is, don't you?"

He nodded, wondering; then was sure.

"You guessed, didn't you," she said. "I didn't tell you, did I?"

Sulgrave was silent a moment, thinking.

"So Dolfus took an interest in the boy because he was your son?"

She caught at a deep breath, looked away from him as though flinching from a slap; gripped tightly in her own embrace, she huddled from some chilling blast of sudden feeling, nodded a quick, bitter nod.

He said nothing, reached out and touched her bare foot.

She looked up, the tremor past. "Mother was very ill," she

said, as though making a small plea. "And Ben was very young then." She abruptly looked away again, whispered brokenly, ". . . just a little younger than you . . ." and covered her face with her hands and cried. She cried like a woman who had forgotten how, sobbing as though she were choking. And when he pulled away her hands and lifted her chin, her face was horrible to look at; enclosed with pain, her ugliness was astonishing: he loved her.

The main load, the largest shipment to date, came in the middle of the week. With the docking of the large ship, the glass began to fall; the radio shack picked up a gale warning. Using a full shift of men, they unloaded all afternoon and halfway into the night. Then, with the sea kicking up, a torpedo swung gently against the side of the hold and killed a man. He died of a fractured skull.

In rising wind and rain, under artificial lights, unloading became difficult. After the accident, very simply, the men refused to unload further. Dolfus was remonstrating with them when, like Moses descending from the mountain, the Commander appeared out of the black-flying rain. He threatened everyone refusing to unload with court-martial for mutiny; half the men had already gone to barracks.

In the barracks was where the real mutiny threatened to erupt, for Hake alternated between cajolery and insult on the theory that anger was the only antidote to fear and fatigue. In the end all went back but six; then Big Randy literally kicked his younger brother out of the barracks and that made five. Randy himself hardly even refused; he just sat down on his bunk and shook his head silently. Orval Blue-Eyes made the error of sticking his head in to see what was going on: Hake said, "You, too, Steward. Even house darkies work during harvest." And Orval, who for all his shuffling disguises was from Detroit, caught by surprise, told Hake, "I ain't your slave, whitefolks," splashed Hake with the pure acid of unconcealed cynicism. Hake called him to attention;

Orval ignored him, went to his bunk and sat down. "I'll salute your flag and polish your buttons, but I won't kiss you' white ass." Dolfus walked out on the Commander in disgust, after calling him a damn fool to his face. It fell to Sulgrave to arrest the six; his embarrassment was enough apology, and they gathered up their things quietly and went with him to the empty ammunition bunker that was designated their prison.

As it turned out, their gesture of rebellion was wasted. In the time they'd been off the pier, the skipper of the ammunition vessel had decided to stand out to sea till the blow was over, preferring the open fury of deep water to the shallow confinement of the bay. The seven-ton topping-lift booms were already secured when Sulgrave returned to the dock, and Hake himself was assisting on the dock as the skipper stood on the wing of the bridge with a megaphone directing the casting off of lines. He didn't cast off his breast spring until last, letting the wind turn the ship clear of the dock before ringing for full astern and completing his turn toward open water. Hake watched the full maneuver critically, nodded his approval, and retired from the dock. Sulgrave worked with the men until dawn, securing the pier. The rising wind and rain made words less effective than gestures. Dolfus was nowhere to be seen; on returning, Sulgrave saw the lighted chow hall, learned that Dolfus had roused the cooks an hour early to have coffee ready for the men.

The wind blew for three days before the ship returned and unloading recommenced. Sulgrave had slipped into the role of self-appointed warder to the men in the bunker. He did what he could to help them make themselves comfortable, brought them a bucket of whitewash to brighten the interior of the rock, supervised their thrice-daily exercise period under guard outside. For the noontime meal, he carried the hot canisters up himself. It was planned that the men would leave with the ship at the end of the week, and it seemed the least he could do temporarily to ease the discomfort of their incarceration. To Sulgrave, for reasons of conscience which he didn't stop to examine, it was a way of atonement.

"You don't think I grieve him?" she asked absently. "You don't think I have a hole inside me because he's gone? He's always been away from me, been away so long that it's hard to realize that this time it's different, that he's never coming back to me."

"Was it the same after . . . after your son . . ."

"It was the same."

"With Dolfus, then?"

"It was with Ben, yes. Severn couldn't stand it. He went away after it, back to duty. Ben was all I had. He was a friend to the boy, and I loved him for that too. Perhaps that's why, I don't know."

"Did he know, your husband?"

"I don't know. I told you—he was jealous of any junior officer who was even polite to me. And yet he was always throwing them in my path. Almost as though . . ."

"To test you?"

". . . as though he wanted me to. I can't explain it. I tried to tell you before. He always seemed to be the entrepreneur, inviting them to stay weekends and then being called away —that happened once with his exec, the one that was with him when the destroyer . . ."

"The one who was adjudged responsible for not keeping his charts up to date?"

"That was the navigation officer. He stayed at the house once too."

"Yet only with Skully . . ."

"I wish you wouldn't call him that. That's a hateful nickname."

"The men gave it to him. I think he liked it. Old Skully."

"His name is Benjamin. Was . . ."

He reached across the pillow and smoothed her forehead. "Don't frown. I'm sorry. It's just that I want to know everything there is to know about you."

She turned toward him like a cat, lightly beating her fists on his shoulders, then gripped him strongly, her ear to his chest as though listening. "I can't help it," she said. "Right now I love you. You're such a beautiful young man. So alive. So alive."

Gently he stroked her hair, stared at the whiteness of the ceiling. "I love you too, old Vanna. I've never needed to love a woman so much before. I'm not sure I even knew what it was."

After a while he said, "I have your letters. I found them after the . . ."

She didn't stir.

"I read them."

She said nothing, gave no sign.

"I also found his sword, the cutlass he said belonged to your father. The blade's broken. Perhaps it can be fixed."

After a long time, so long that, drowsing himself, he thought she'd fallen asleep, she said, "My father hated him. I had to make him go to his bachelor's dinner and promise to give a toast. Do you know what his toast was?"

"No."

"He said, 'This sword goes with my daughter.' And handed it to him across the table blade first."

After that she said nothing more, and later, in the failing afternoon of December sun, followed him down the long tunnel of sleep and love.

In the days and nights that followed, they dredged each other's intimate history as though compelled to confess and to know, dragging beneath the bright surface of childhood memories to murky depths of adult secrets; and found in each other an endless reflection of each self, a strangely comforting renewal of life and knowledge. They took their meals in the suite, played word games cheating like children, and double solitaire, even once hide-and-seek, naked, in the dark. There was a radio, a station that played symphonies all night, and they listened to music lying on the plush carpet with pillows. There was never any thought or suggestion of going out, except once, on Wednesday, when she went out while he was sleeping—to buy him a razor.

And she even confessed that for one unbearable minute she'd wanted to kill him—when he had told her of reading her letters.

LT. BEN DOLFUS PUT THIS HERE
MCMXLI
HE SAYS HELLO

On Wednesday morning he was still sleeping when she left a note and slipped out to buy the razor. It was not the appearance of his three-day beard that bothered her, but rather its increasing abrasiveness on her own skin. Also, she knew, she rather looked forward to watching him shave; it had always given her a mysterious physical pleasure to watch the ritual of a man shaving, and she wondered about this as she hurried out of the hotel into the brisk morning street. She distinctly remembered her father, who had had his shaving water brought to him each morning in a brass can with a hot towel over it; and she remembered her husband, who had shaved with such reckless haste that he was forever nicking himself. Her father was slow and methodical, never had to have recourse to the styptic pencil. The way a man shaved, she thought, reflected the inner design of his life. But I really haven't watched enough men to be sure. I never saw Ben shave. She hurried along the sidewalk feeling pleasure as well as purpose in her errand. She felt good, pleased at the thought that for the first time in years she was out on the streets without her lipstick on.

The razor was quickly bought in a drugstore on the corner. She also bought three new lipsticks, each a different color, nothing near the colors she usually wore. She told the clerk not to wrap the articles, paid, and put them in her purse. Leaving the drugstore, she crossed the street and on impulse made for a bench in the small park diagonally opposite her hotel. She sat down, wanting simply to relax by herself and to enjoy for a moment, before going back, the meager warmth of the chill November sun. Across the street, the angled façades of the hotel met and rose like the prow of an enormous ship bearing directly down on her.

She counted up the floors, trying to locate the room. The room. She thought of his jacket hanging over the chair, with its two gold stripes too new yet to be tarnished. Not a lamb any more, but still innocent. The thought of him sleeping in her own hired bed made her feel for an instant's twinge like a spoiler, yet victorious. What am I? He's old enough to be his own man. His beard scratches like a man's beard. She smiled to herself and touched her own cheek, remembering the erotic stir inside her.

Suddenly she felt an immense flood of tenderness for everything around her. Dear hotel, she thought. Dear tree. Dear old bench in the park. Get thee with child . . . wonder what a mandrake root is. Man. Drake and duck? Root?

Would I have the courage to have it if I were? I have the courage right this minute. I feel good. I want to *be* good. Be all good.

Two small children, a boy and a girl, were playing with a pile of sticks on the bench next to hers. They were lining up the sticks by wedging them between the slats in the back of the bench. Following her impulse to act, she opened her purse and took out a package of peppermints. She felt almost giddy with pleasure.

"Would you children like a candy?"

The children didn't move, didn't even look at her.

"They're peppermints. Do you like peppermints? They have holes in them. If you have some string, you can make a bracelet . . ."

Suddenly, unaccountably, the two children turned and ran off to join another group playing skiprope under the supervision of a large woman in a plain felt hat. The woman saw what had happened; immediately she detached herself from the group and came over toward her. She rose to meet the woman; sitting down seemed to be a disadvantage.

"I—I thought they might like peppermint," she began when the woman was close enough to hear. She felt unstrung, vaguely accused.

"You mustn't be upset," the woman said. "It's just that they're deaf. I'll be glad to give them the candy. They didn't hear you."

As she crossed the street she felt near to tears, and in the very middle of the light stream of traffic she stopped and looked up but couldn't find the window again. Suddenly she was assailed by the panicky thought that he had awakened. He'd failed to see the note and had gone out. Run out? Ridiculous. He would hardly have had time to dress. Foolishness. The moment passed. But she hurried across the street without even looking, and by the time she reached the revolving doors she was slightly breathless and her heart was pounding.

When she entered the room it was just as she'd left it. The temperature was the same; the smell, the light was the same. The note was on the rug where she'd left it, untouched. She snatched it up and crumpled it, as though to destroy the evidence of her absence. Silently she tiptoed through the bedroom into the bathroom; there she removed her clothes. She wanted terribly to be back in bed before he awakened. I shouldn't have gone out. What am I afraid of? Foolishness. Foolishness of age. But it might have broken the spell. Age, she thought, and looked at her face in the mirror. I need him. I'm not strong enough to stand on my own two feet alone yet. Age. Do I look old to him?

She raised her hands to her cheeks to stretch out the tiny

wrinkles. Hands. Not my face. My hands. Age. My hands will be my first betrayers.

Suddenly she laughed at herself in the mirror. You've got a young squire asleep in your bed, and you worry about your hands. Foolishness of age, dear girl. She picked a lipstick at random from her purse and started to freshen her lips, stopped midway and looked at her left hand again, and laughed. "You traitor," she whispered. "Do you know what happens to traitors?" Amused at herself, she made a carmine slash across her wrist with the lipstick. Very funny, she thought sarcastically of herself. Now you'll have to scrub it off. She gazed at the bright wrist. Enough silliness. Dulce et decorum est, pro patria morior, she thought. She hummed a tune as she washed her lipstick off. Enough. To bed, to bed.

When he awoke in the morning, he remembered only the desperate eerie fury of what had seemed the final procreative act, and blocked it out of memory as though it had never happened:

Dolfus was restricted to the Rock, so Sulgrave had taken the Goldilocks doll over to Little Misery; Dolfus warned him to give it to Arielle when Mother-in-Trouble wasn't around, since the girl had had a white doll before and the old woman, for dark reasons of her own, had destroyed it, burned it in the stove.

When Arielle received the doll she was delighted, and he helped her find a hiding place for it up under the boards beneath the shack.

"If I give you babee, you take me to New York?" she asked.

He smiled and said that perhaps someday.

He thought no more about it until late that night when he awakened with her already in his bed. Dolfus was on watch.

And the young smell of her
God yes, the smell of her

On Friday he awoke to find her lying on her side watching him. Some particularly disturbing dream had awakened him, nothing to do with her.

"Did you know that you have a pulse at the base of your neck?" she asked. "I've been watching it."

"Good morning," he said without moving. "Or is it afternoon?"

"Your body is hard all over except for this one little hollow here." She touched him lightly between the neck and collarbone. "It shows when men wear open shirts. They seem so vulnerable there."

She stroked his neck lightly with her fingernail. He closed his eyes and fell back into pursuit of the dream that had awakened him.

When he awoke again she was not beside him. He heard the water running in the bath. Immediately he began collecting the fugitive pieces of the dream. It was about Randy. Big Randy. He'd been asking Randy to do a favor, to lie for him. Why couldn't he picture his face? He was big; he had a vague picture of the shape of him, and of the slow way in which he shook his head no. He could hear the cadence of his voice. But he couldn't recall precisely what Randy looked like. He saw Lace clearly, even to the silver ring on his card-player's hand. But Randy remained vague. There seemed something mysterious in that, as though Randy presented a problem that was crucially important to solve.

As he became wider awake the immediacy of the dream

wore off. Whatever message there might have been was lost. The sense of urgency of the waking moment vanished and left in its place an unfamiliar feeling of garish uneasiness that wouldn't shake off, a rootless anxiety utterly new to him.

He lay on his back and stared at the ceiling, his hands behind his head. There's no meaning in it, he thought. He was acutely aware of the sounds from the bath. How could Hake not have enjoyed her? And Hake was dead. Skully must have loved her somehow. And Skully was dead. I've been where they've been, he thought. I've tasted every inch of her. Nothing's happened to me. I am what's happened to me. I am nothing. And I'm better off.

Vaguely his mind registered a change in the sound from the bath: the water was running out of the tub. He closed his eyes and went needlessly back to sleep. The last thing he thought of was Skully and Hake—what were they each thinking when they died? Did they think of each other? Skully said once that Hake had a Samson complex . . .

Down the fugitive alley of another dream: *balled as a bat, blind as an egg, here we go marching headlong headstrong headshorn Uncle Samsson, content to pull the temple down arrears . . .*

The amphibian circled down from the west out of a bleeding sunset, and landed in the milky blue bay just as the seven survivors started down the hill toward where the dock had once been. In that stripped and blackened landscape they looked like pallbearers descending with their burden into hell, for among the twisted wreckage embracing the bay fires still burned. Wooden structures had vanished with the trees, leaving not a hint of their existence; only steel and concrete remained to mark out ruins. The air was hot and still, and all the earth around was cracked and ruptured where raw gigantic handfuls had been ripped skyward. Down below, where nearly all the men had been, there was not much evidence of death except in bits and pieces. The rock had been plowed open as though by God.

The plane crew secured their anchors and came ashore in two emergency rescue rafts. They brought with them lighting equipment, and used the last minutes of fast reddening twilight to set up light poles and generators on what was left of the pad of concrete that had once been the foot of the dock.

It was slow and treacherous going for the group coming down the obliterated path from Commander's country, and in the thickening nightfall the seven survivors were at first unnoticed from below. It wasn't till one of the crew yanked the starter cord of the first generator that the rest of them paused in their task to look about; with the rising putter of the generator, the glowing floods came on. They flung their feeblish garish light across the dead immensity of destruction, and the men of the aircrew saw the seven sole survivors bearing the awkward oversized coffin of the Commander. They were coming down slowly, picking their way; seven men in macabre procession, a funeral without mourners. No one moved. No one spoke. The generator puttered like a dotted line through the ghastly silence of white light.

When the box was set down, like a gift at the rescuers' feet, still no one moved. Finally Sulgrave spoke. He addressed no one, simply stood looking down at the death at his feet, and said, "The Commander."

A silence. Then the Warrant-pilot said, "We'll put him aboard in the morning." Then he said, "We have a doctor . . ."

"Don't need no doctor," Big Randy said sharply.

The doctor stepped forward. "How many bodies are . . ."

A snort of impatience interrupted him. It was then that Lace first said what he would say many times again before this day was forgotten. "Most of them cats got buried in thin air," he said. "Left nothin' behind but footprints."

Randy suddenly turned his back and sat down hard on the Commander's box, stumbling as though dizzy. He put his head in his hands and rocked himself slowly like a man doubled over in pain. This time, as he cried, he didn't make a sound.

It was just before they boarded the plane the morning after the blast—the amphibian had remained in the bay during the night—that he learned of Randy's macabre revenge for his younger brother's death. By then the coffin was already loaded aboard the plane. It was Orval who spilled the beans.

He'd taken Orval with him to make one last-ditch search for the sword in the wreckage that was the Commander's quarters. It was when he told Orval what he was particularly searching for that Orval began skirting around the question of the body. Would they open it before they buried him? Would they ask who put him in dress whites?

Finally Sulgrave squared the steward with one question: "What's wrong, Orval?"

Guilt was too plain in Orval's face for Sulgrave to accept his "Ain't nuthin' wrong, sir. I was just asking."

It took some doing, and some threatening questions. But finally Orval couldn't contain his fear of divine retribution. "Randy don't fear none of the Lord, Lieutenant. I ain't very religious myself. But when it comes to buryin' . . ."

And then it came out that they couldn't find all of the Commander, only the head and upper torso. The rest they'd made up with assorted arms and legs, some white, some black. "They might sure be a piece of Mister Skully in that suit, Lieutenant. We put in all the Commander we could find, though."

Sulgrave, jolted, hid his own sudden awed chill, said nothing while he tried to figure out the possible consequences. They resumed the search more intensively, while to himself he asked Orval's questions. In the end they found the sword, broken, under a rock.

When Lace and Randy came back from Little Misery, where Sulgrave had sent them to check on the state of things, Sulgrave said nothing about the body for the moment.

"Mr. Sung got 'em all off in the schooner. He didn't know but what there'd be a second blast after the first," Randy said.

"Mr. Sung is still there?" Sulgrave asked, astounded.

"He's pickin' up the coconuts off his place. They all got shook down," Lace said.

179

He'd never seen a full-grown woman so defeated. She was actually on her knees before him toward the end. But the news broadcast had told him enough for both of them to know that his leave was canceled, and nothing she could do —smashing the radio, crying, cursing him, begging him— could change even then what they both knew overshadowed their life in the room together.

"Every man I've ever loved killed, God damn it." She plucked at the rug as though uprooting grass. "Every one of them. My son. My . . ."

"Please get up. Please get up. I've got to check in. You know I'll be back."

"You'll never come back. Just a few days longer, please."

He laughed, trying to jolly away her hysteria. "You know I've at least got to present myself. I might be assigned right here, who knows?"

"But just a few more days. Please, please."

"But why? I can come back as soon as . . ."

She rocked from side to side on her knees, held her fists to her temples. "I don't know," she whispered hoarsely. "I'm crazy. Please don't laugh at me. *I want to have a baby. Please, God, don't laugh at me. I wasn't sure before.*"

He didn't laugh. He was struck dumb. An overmastering sense of tenderness, pity, panic, love—he couldn't separate the tangled snarl of conflicting feelings—brought him to one knee beside her. She was crying easily now, head bent, the back of her hand in her mouth. He lifted the soft hair off the back of her neck and gently bit the nape. "I love you," he said.

He tried to lift her but she shook him off. "Go," she said harshly. "Get out."

He rose and took his coat over his arm, feeling wrong and harsh in the clothes he hadn't worn for so long. He looked back only once, as he closed the door. She was still crying, head bowed, blindly waving him to go on, to leave quickly. She was wearing the same feminine spill of white froth and ribboned ivory lace that she'd been wearing that morning of another century. She looked like a weeping angel. A dull senseless helpless misery came over him as he closed the door, and everything inside him turned to stone.

"Did you go to Mother-in-Trouble's?"

"Yeah," Lace said. "The shack stood up, but everything else is a mess." He shook his head, remembering. "Twisted scene. You know that turpentine tree in the yard there?"

Sulgrave nodded.

"There's a yella-haired doll hanging from it. Hung by the neck."

The old woman, he thought dully.

As they left, the radio operator of the amphibian received a message that two rescue ships had been sent, were within two hours of the island. When they took off, Sulgrave had the pilot circle the island before they gained altitude. From the air the two converging ships were visible in the binoculars. "They won't have much rescuing to do," the radio man said, shaking his head.

"Got a lot of cleaning up," Lace said.

She stood before the mirror dry-eyed and exhausted, numb to further feeling. She studied herself, her face. It was wan, terribly drawn from crying. Slowly she opened her lipstick, twisting the brass tube till the carmine tip emerged erect, very deliberately made up her mouth. Then she reached for her brush, absently started brushing her hair, wondering again if there were life in her womb. Sunday, she thought, today is Sunday.

Sulgrave came out of the hotel into the evening street as though coming once again into the world. It was a winter feeling he remembered from boyhood, of coming out of the Saturday matinée movie, of coming out into the bustle and bitter darkness of evening after having entered in the bright cold sunshine of afternoon. And in that instant he wondered if he would come through it alive. He remembered Vanna's last words as he left, but something within him brushed them aside. He thought of Vanna herself, and in that moment was mistakenly—it was always a mistake to be sure of the future—mistakenly certain he'd survive. The first thing that really struck his vision was a newspaper; a fur-coated woman was carrying it, reading as she walked. The tabloid bore a single six-inch black headline:

WAR

The word should have fallen on his life like a cleaver. It was absurd. He thought of Dolfus. He thought of the last thing he'd seen as they circled to set a course away from the island. Laughing Boy. The gigantic statue had looked small from the air, and even smaller as the ludicrous weeping features were obliterated in distance. He remembered watching it and holding his breath so as not to fog the cold plastic window, watching until even the spot where that statue stood was lost in hazy reflection of morning sun and sea.

H. L. "DOC" HUMES (1926–1992) was one of the originators of *The Paris Review* and the author of two novels, *The Underground City* and *Men Die.* His third novel, *The Memoirs of Dorsey Slade,* was never completed. He lived in Paris and Greenwich Village. Doc is also the subject of a documentary being produced by the Academy Award–nominated filmmaker Immy Humes, his daughter.

For further information, please visit www.dochumes.com.